PROMISE FROM
A COWBOY

———

C.J. CARMICHAEL

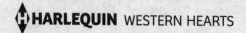

Recycling programs
for this product may
not exist in your area.

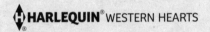

HARLEQUIN® WESTERN HEARTS

ISBN-13: 978-1-335-50801-0

Promise from a Cowboy
First published in 2013.
This edition published in 2020.
Copyright © 2013 by Carla Daum

This edition published by arrangement with Harlequin Books S.A.

For questions and comments about the quality of this book, please contact us at CustomerService@Harlequin.com.

Harlequin Enterprises ULC
22 Adelaide St. West, 40th Floor
Toronto, Ontario M5H 4E3, Canada
www.Harlequin.com

Printed in U.S.A.

Hard to imagine a more glamorous life than being an accountant, isn't it? Still, **C.J. Carmichael** gave up the thrills of income tax forms and double-entry bookkeeping when she sold her first book in 1998. She has now written more than thirty-five novels for Harlequin and invites you to learn more about her books, see photos of her hiking exploits and enter her surprise contests at cjcarmichael.com.

This is for my writing companion,
my real "lap-top," our family cat Penny.
Every writer should have a classy cat like you.

Prologue

Sheriff Savannah Moody drove up to the church and parked right at the front, next to the bridal party's white sedan. She thought of all the people waiting inside. The white steeple was the visual focal point of Coffee Creek, Montana, but Savannah had rarely been inside.

Her father's funeral, with the paltry attendance of less than a dozen mourners, the marriage of a close friend and then that friend's first baby's christening. That was pretty much it.

And now this.

With long, purposeful strides, she made her way along the sidewalk, up the stairs and to the double doors. Muffled organ music seeped out from the building's pores—a joyous sound that soon would end.

Delivering tragic news was the hardest part of her job. Today she had to do it to a man who'd been her first love. They'd dated all through high school. She'd been so sure she'd spend the rest of her life with him.

Then he'd done something stupid, involved her brother, and the next thing she knew he'd joined the rodeo circuit, rarely making it home to Coffee Creek in the seventeen years that followed.

But he was home now. She'd seen his truck in town a few times this week. He'd returned to witness the marriage of his youngest brother, Brock.

Savannah swallowed, then took a deep breath and went in.

The organ music swelled, became something she recognized, but couldn't name. The chatter of the waiting guests was cheerful, but edged with anxiety. Judging by the number of vehicles parked outside, at least a hundred people were waiting inside. But the vestibule was empty, so she continued toward two open doors to her right.

She'd no sooner stepped onto the blue carpet that stretched the length of the aisle, when sudden silence fell over the church. A hundred smiling, curious faces turned to face her.

They were expecting the bride.

Instead, they saw the local sheriff. And in that second expressions changed to worry, shock, concern...and fear.

"I need to talk to someone from the Lambert family." Savannah thought her voice sounded too loud in the silent church. Sensing movement behind her, she turned to see the bridal party approaching from the rear.

First was the dark-haired bride, Winnie Hays, owner of the Cinnamon Stick Café.

Savannah had never met the redheaded bridesmaid standing a step behind Winnie, but she'd heard that a best friend from New York City had arrived in town a week ago to participate in the festivities. So this was obviously her.

The second bridesmaid was Brock's blonde sister, Cassidy. She looked so pale, Savannah was worried she was about to faint.

Savannah turned back to the front of the church where the rest of the Lambert family was seated. Olive, matriarch of the largest ranch in the county since her husband's death many years ago, had never hidden the fact that she looked down on Savannah and her family. Beside her was her eldest son,

B.J. His eyes were on her and the penetrating gray gaze suddenly became the only thing she could focus on.

B.J. was the first to stand, so handsome and civilized in his dark gray suit. "Savannah. What happened?"

Olive stood up next, using her son's arm for support. "Has there been an accident?"

"I'm sorry, Olive. But yes." She had to push herself to add, "There's been an a-accident. Jackson's SUV hit a moose on Big Valley Road, about five miles from town."

A collective gasp by the congregation was followed by a few seconds of stunned silence.

"Brock?" Winnie asked from behind her, voice trembling.

Savannah turned to face the bride. "I'm so sorry, Winnie. Brock was sitting in the front passenger seat—the impact point with the moose. He didn't have a chance."

Savannah knew the pain her words were causing and she hated it. She called on all her strength to keep calm and measured.

And then B.J. was speaking again. "What about Corb? And Jackson?"

Jackson had been taken in by the Lamberts when he was thirteen years old. And Corb was the third Lambert son, the next oldest after B.J.

"Jackson was driving, wearing his seat belt, and the air bag was able to cushion him from the worst of it. He's badly bruised and shaken, but he's okay. Corb was in the backseat. He should have been fine, but I'm afraid he wasn't wearing his seat belt. As we speak he's being medevaced to Great Falls. I can't say how bad his injuries are. You'll have to talk to the doctors about that."

"Is he conscious?" B.J.'s mother asked, her eyes wide with desperation.

Again Savannah shook her head, wishing there were some way to cushion the blow. "No."

Overcome, finally, by the shock and the horror, the bride swayed and suddenly everyone was rushing forward to help.

"We need a sweater, or a warm jacket," the redheaded bridesmaid called out to the crowd.

A second later, a man's suit jacket was settled over Winnie's shoulders and Dan Farley, the local vet, was ordering the crowd to step back and give Winnie some space. The large, muscular man then picked up the bride and carried her out for some fresh air.

Savannah switched into crowd-control mode and cleared a path for Farley, the bride and the bridesmaid to exit the church. Then she supervised the orderly evacuation of the rest of the Lambert family.

B.J.'s gaze fell on hers as he passed by. Her stomach clenched at the fear and worry on his face. She almost reached out her arm to him. Then drew it back.

Once, she could have provided him comfort. But those days were over.

Chapter 1

Eleven months later

B.J. Lambert was in the loading chute at the Wild Rogue Rodeo in Central Point, Oregon, about to settle all one hundred and sixty pounds of himself on the back of a horse that had been named Bucking Machine.

These were the moments B.J. lived for. As he clamped down on the adrenaline rush of anticipation and fear—and yes, there was fear, only a fool wouldn't have at least a little—a deep calm washed over him.

Once that chute was opened, it would all be over in eight seconds. He might have the best ride of his life or be disqualified. He could end up injured, or he might stroll out of the arena as nonchalantly as if he'd just taken a walk through a park.

B.J. pulled in as much air as his lungs could hold. He knew the announcer was talking about his accomplishments, perhaps going so far as to call him one of the legends of rodeo.

After eighteen years on the circuit, the buckles and trophies tended to add up.

But B.J. wasn't listening to any of that. His mind was focused entirely on the present and the animal he was about to ride.

"Give me your best," he said in a low voice to Bucking Machine. "And I'll give you mine."

He gripped the rigging in his left hand and gave the signal he was ready. As the chute opened he settled his full weight on the gelding and the ride began.

Bucking Machine started with a wild leap and B.J. focused on making contact with the heels of his boots, marking him out to prevent disqualification.

Then, with his right hand high in the air, he matched his wits, strength and balance with those of the horse. He wasn't so much thinking at this point as simply doing what came naturally.

The more wicked turns and kicks the horse

threw at him, the happier B.J. was. Only 50 percent of his grade was based on his skills—the rest was up to the gelding.

Give me all you've got. I can take it.

And he did. But when the eight-second horn sounded, he lost no time in getting off. He jumped, managing to land on his feet in the dirt-packed arena.

From the volume of the crowd's cheering, he could tell he'd had a good round. He waved his hat, specifically looking for his sister, Cassidy, and her fiancé, Dan Farley, who were also participating in the rodeo. Next he looked for his mother, sitting rigidly in the stands.

Olive did not approve of the rodeo and he didn't kid himself that she was here to watch him perform. No, she'd driven all this way to cheer on Cassidy and Farley, whose recent engagement had pleased her so much she was willing to put aside her usual distaste for the sport.

The engagement was good news for a family that had had a hell of a rough ride this year. After Brock's death, it had seemed nothing would ever be right again. The loss always hit B.J. hardest at night—he hadn't had a straight eight hours of sleep in a long time.

But he was grateful that Corb had recov-

ered from his injuries. He'd even fallen in
love and married Laurel Sheridan, Winnie's
red-haired friend from New York City. Now
they had a little daughter—life continued.

Winnie, however, still hadn't returned to
Coffee Creek since Brock's funeral. She was
convalescing at her parents' farm in the Highwood area. The family had been shocked to
learn that she'd been two months pregnant
at the time of the accident. Now she had a
little boy and B.J. wondered when he would
meet him.

He'd called Winnie a few times since
Brock's death. Their conversations were always short, since neither of them knew quite
what to say. They always ended the same way,
with Winnie promising to return with her son
to Coffee Creek one day soon.

But in the meantime, her staff and Laurel
were running the Cinnamon Stick Café.

As for Jackson, nothing anyone said
seemed able to lessen the guilt he felt for
being the driver that day. B.J. felt bad for his
foster brother and hoped that eventually time
would heal his pain.

B.J. himself was no stranger to guilt. He
knew that with Brock gone, it was up to him,
the eldest son, to step in and help. But the
rodeo had become more than a job to him

over the years. It was an adrenaline addiction that kept him from thinking of a certain woman he should have forgotten a long time ago.

He gave his head a shake and reminded himself to focus. Lately his thoughts had been scattering far too easily.

"…and we have an eighty-nine for Mr. B. J. Lambert today, ladies and gentlemen. That pretty much guarantees him top standing for the Wild Rogue this year. Give it up, folks, for a gentleman who has dedicated many good years to this sport we all love…"

Tommy, one of the pick-up men, clapped his shoulder. "Well done." A couple other competitors offered their congratulations, too, stopping him to shake his hand and make admiring comments about his ride.

Once upon a time B.J. would have enjoyed all of this. Winning was the point, right?

But today he felt flat. That moment in the chute with Bucking Machine had meant more to him than any of this.

And later, when he was called to the stage and given his check and trophy, it was all he could do to muster a smile and wave at the spectators.

His sister came running and threw out her

arms for a big hug. "Way to go, B.J. We're all so proud of you."

Her fiancé, a man who had been his friend since they were mutton-busting age, gave him a firm handshake. "Impressive. Hell, you were the man to beat, but no one even came close."

B.J. shrugged. "It's what I do. You novices, though, you really kicked butt. You're the ones who deserve the big congratulations."

Cassidy flushed. She'd come in third in barrel racing after a six-year hiatus from the sport, while Farley, a full-time vet who competed only occasionally in the rodeo, had managed to take first place in steer wrestling. B.J. could tell he was still on a high from his great performance. B.J. remembered well the days when winning had made him feel that way, too.

Hard to say when the thrill had started to fade. Maybe when he'd noticed the other cowboys sharing their victories with girlfriends, wives and children, while he always stood on the podium alone?

"We were *all* pretty awesome," Cassidy said, linking one arm around Farley, the other around her brother. His sister looked happier than he'd seen her in some time, and he was glad for her. She'd recently decided to leave behind her planned business career to work as a horse trainer and teacher with Straws Monahan. Her recent engagement to Farley was also a big reason for the glow in her smile.

"You two make a great couple," he said.

And that's when his mother joined the group. She was decked out in a stylish skirt and trimmed Western shirt, looking spry and fit for a woman in her sixties.

"You did well, Robert James." The words were right, but the tone held the note of contained disapproval that he was used to hearing from his mother.

"Thanks, Mom. I'm glad you could be here."

She nodded, then turned to her daughter. "I'm tired. Think I'll head back to the hotel."

"Oh." Cassidy's face fell. "Would you like us to come with you?"

"No. You go ahead and celebrate." She sighed. It was the drinking and partying that accompanied rodeo that she most disapproved of. "I suppose you've earned the right to a little fun."

"We'll have fun," Cassidy agreed. "But you know we won't overdo the drinking. We never do."

B.J. wondered if his sister thought she was

speaking for him, too, when she said that. If so, she wasn't being entirely honest.

"Ready to head over to the Rogue Saloon?" Cassidy asked him, once their mother had departed.

"I'll meet you there. I promised an interview to a reporter from the *Mail Tribune*." His sister didn't look too disappointed, and neither did Farley. He was definitely the third wheel tonight. Maybe he'd just skip the party. He wasn't much in the mood, anyway.

It turned out there were a couple of reporters waiting to interview him, and he answered their questions politely, giving the stock answers that he had memorized years ago.

He'd thought he was finished, when he felt a tap on his shoulder.

"B.J.?"

The nerves that ran along his spine tingled at the sound of her voice.

He turned slowly, taking the time for a good long look before he answered. Savannah—the local sheriff back home—wasn't in uniform tonight. She was wearing her thick, dark hair long, and in her jeans, brown boots and black-and-gray shirt, she could have been just another pretty rodeo fan.

She had on silver hoop earrings and a silver star that hung from her neck by a black ribbon. But what really drew his gaze were her eyes, dark and wary.

"How are you, Savannah?" He almost couldn't believe it was really her. For eighteen years she'd barely spoken to him—except when official duty required her to, like the day his brother Brock had died.

She shrugged, as if to say it didn't matter how she was.

"Something's happened," she said.

His heart contracted painfully. "Not another accident."

"No." She held out her hand in a reassuring gesture. "No. Nothing like that. It's about the fire."

He understood immediately that she was referring to the awful night that had changed everything between them. She'd been home babysitting her little sister while he went out partying with their friends and her twin brother, Hunter.

Right from the beginning things had gone wrong. First the location. Hunter had been keen for their group to ride ATVs out to an abandoned barn on Olive's estranged sister's property. B.J. hadn't felt right about it, but he'd gone along.

Then a big electrical storm had struck, spooking the girls and sending them running. Only Brock and Hunter had stayed behind to witness the barn catching fire. Not until later did they discover that a vagrant had been passed out in the loft. Rain had put out the fire before the barn burned down, but smoke inhalation killed the vagrant.

B.J. had been the one to insist on calling the authorities. He'd also done what he thought was the noble thing—taking the blame for inviting his friends out to his aunt's barn. He'd wanted to protect his girlfriend's brother, not ever considering that Savannah would blame him for getting Hunter in trouble.

"Isn't that ancient history?"

"I wish." She exhaled her annoyance. "I had a visit from a private investigator from L.A." She frowned as a young man carrying two beers in his hands jostled her shoulder. "Could we find someplace quiet to talk?"

He thought about his trailer. Too small, too intimate. The saloon where Cassidy and Farley were headed would be noisy. "I could stand some food. Want to go out for a steak?"

She hesitated, and he could see the mistrust in her eyes. Even after all these years, it hurt.

She blamed him for what had happened to her brother. Always a kid who invited trouble, Hunter had grown even wilder after the fire. He'd given up on school, found a rougher set of friends, and two months later, on his and Savannah's eighteenth birthday, had stolen money from their mother and run off to his first rodeo.

Since then he'd been traveling from one state to the other, always on the move.

On the surface—and to Savannah—it probably seemed as if he and Hunter lived pretty similar lives. But the heavy drinking and gambling that sucked up most of Hunter's energy was not B.J.'s scene.

"My truck is parked close." She pointed to the visitor lot. "How about we talk there?"

Though she worded it as a question, she didn't wait for him to answer—just started walking as if she expected him to follow.

B.J. stood his ground. Following wasn't something he did a lot of. But this was Savannah and he had to hear what was on her mind. With a sigh, he set off after her.

Savannah could feel her phone vibrating as she moved away from B. J. Lambert. Good. She needed a distraction.

As soon as she'd started talking to him, she'd realized approaching B.J. was a mistake. She'd thought enough years had passed that he would be almost like a stranger to her now. But strangers—not even the best-looking ones—didn't make her palms sweat.

She was a sheriff, damn it. She was supposed to be *tough*.

She'd come to the rodeo in the first place hoping to see her brother. But though he was registered, Hunter hadn't shown up.

A typical Hunter move. And since he refused to own a cell phone, she had no easy way to locate him.

Talking to B.J. had been the logical next step. Until she'd looked into those knowing gray eyes of his and had felt all her insides come undone.

As she reached for her phone, she hoped B.J. would get stubborn and refuse to cooperate. But she could hear the sound of his boots scuffing along the hard-packed dirt behind her.

She'd started something now. The Lord only knew where it would end.

Savannah glanced at her phone's display, hoping the call would be official business requiring her to leave Central Point, Oregon, right this minute. But the number was from the Mountain View Care Home back in Coffee Creek.

"Savannah Moody."

"I can't find my slippers."

She tried not to sigh. The staff at the care home had been instructed to restrict her mother's calls. But Francine Moody could be ingenious, and no one appreciated that better than Savannah.

Over the years her mother's calls had become increasingly frequent and ever more muddled. Francine had never had the strongest hold on reality. Now it was mostly beyond her grasp.

"Mom, hang up the phone and ask Aubrey to help you find them."

"Who's Aubrey?"

"She feeds you dinner every evening, remember? The nice woman with the smile you say reminds you of Goldie Hawn?"

Actually, aside from her dyed blond hair and winning smile, Aubrey looked nothing like the winsome movie star. But the association seemed to help her mom's failing memory.

"Oh, yes, Goldie Hawn. Do you remember when she—"

"Mom, I've got to go now, okay?" If she let her ramble on, her mother would spend the next thirty minutes rehashing the plot of some old movie. "I'll be home again in a few days and I'll visit you then." She closed her phone, hoping B.J. hadn't heard any of that.

His pity about her down-and-out family was the last thing she needed.

A few steps away from her truck, Savannah pulled out her keys and clicked the unlock button. She'd just slid behind the steering wheel, when B.J. plopped himself right next to her.

She stared straight ahead, trying to adjust to his presence. But even without looking she could sense his long, muscular form beside her.

B.J. was too tall to be a cowboy, but that hadn't stopped him from being a success at it. He had a high forehead and a strong jaw and chin, and intense gray eyes that hinted at green when the light was right.

From the first time she'd met him—at age fifteen when she'd walked into class as the new kid in town—she'd thought he was the best-looking guy she'd ever seen.

She still thought that.

Reluctantly.

Asking him to come to her truck had been a mistake. She'd thought a restaurant would be too intimate. But her cab had never felt so small, and if there'd been a table between them, at least she wouldn't have had to sit so close that their shoulders practically touched.

The table also would have hidden the long

line of his jean-clad thigh. And surely, in a restaurant, she wouldn't have been able to hear the sound of him breathing.

"This is real cozy, but an open window would be nice."

Quickly she inserted the key, then powered down both windows. "Sorry. This is awkward."

"It doesn't have to be, Savannah."

Was he serious? She had to check his expression to be sure, but he didn't seem to be mocking her.

"I heard your mom was in the care home in town now. How is she adjusting?"

So he *had* heard the call. Damn.

"Pretty good. Half the time she doesn't really understand where she is, anyway."

"That's got to be tough."

Savannah shrugged. Life with her mother had always been tough. Francine had been a flighty parent and an erratic housekeeper. But only recently had she crossed the line and become careless to the point of causing harm. Two years ago she'd flooded the main floor bathroom of their home on a twenty-acre plot of land just outside of town. The next month she'd almost set the house on fire.

"Do the doctors think she has Alzheimer's?"

"No. She remembers some things just fine. She can tell you the exact year she planted each of the perennials in the garden at home. She's just got…really bad judgment when it comes to everyday decisions. Her doctor insisted that she needed round-the-clock care, and since I can hardly afford that, there was no option but to send her away."

Savannah did her best not to sound bitter. But it wasn't easy, knowing that if Olive Lambert ever got really sick, her kids would have no trouble affording top-notch medical care.

At one time the discrepancy between the Lamberts and the Moodys hadn't bothered her at all.

But that was before her brother's future had been compromised by a prank that had turned into a full-blown disaster. On the surface it didn't seem that bad. A bunch of foolish high school kids trespassing in an old barn and having an underage drinking party.

It wasn't their fault the storm had blown in. Or that lightning had struck, setting the barn on fire.

But the presence of that vagrant in the loft troubled Savannah. It seemed too much of a coincidence. There had to be more to the story than either B.J. or her brother was letting on.

"What about Regan?" B.J. asked, continuing his polite inquiries about her family. "I heard she graduated from the University of Montana this year, same as my sister, Cassidy."

Savannah couldn't help but perk up at the mention of her ten-year-younger sister. "She sure did. She's applied to medical school, too." Every day Savannah checked the mail with a hope that bordered on desperation. She so much wanted her baby sister to have the success and respect that she deserved.

Unlike their brother, Regan had always been easy to manage. She excelled at school, never broke the rules that her sister set for her and was helpful at home, doing most of the cooking—a job Savannah disliked.

"She'll make a great doctor," B.J. said. "Remember how she was always trying to patch up those dolls of hers?"

Savannah started to smile as she recalled the makeshift beds with their bandaged dolls that Regan would line up on the porch railing when she played "hospital." But the memories, although happy, only reminded her of the special role B.J. had once played in her life.

He'd been around a lot in those days. Regan had almost considered him a second brother.

While she…well, she had considered him something a lot more intimate than that.

She rubbed her temple. Last thing she wanted was to rehash the night everything had changed. Unfortunately, she didn't have a choice. "Like I was saying, I had a visit from a private investigator from Los Angeles last week."

"Yeah?" B.J. sounded cautious.

"The investigator—her name is June Savage—was hired by a wealthy man named Morgan McBride eighteen years ago to find his runaway teenage son, Travis."

B.J. twisted, spreading out his left arm along the back of the seat. She had his full attention now. "So we're talking about our last year of high school?"

He'd done the math and come up with the right answer.

"Yes. Savage never did find the kid—well, not exactly a kid, he was nineteen years old when he went missing. But a few weeks ago a watch came up for sale on eBay. The watch was a McBride heirloom that hadn't been seen since Travis ran away."

"This is sounding complicated."

She agreed. "Savage went to talk to the man who was selling the watch. Turns out he'd bought it at a pawn shop in Lewistown. Want to guess the year?"

"Our graduation year?"

"Right on the first try."

B.J. frowned. "Are you saying this kid was the man who died in the fire?"

"Might be."

"I've always wondered who he was." B.J.'s voice sounded raw.

Savannah nodded. So had she. "Finding that watch caused June Savage to reopen her investigation. Previously she'd been concentrating her search in Mexico, since there had been signs pointing in that direction. This was the first time they considered Montana."

"Montana is one thing. How did Savage narrow it down to Coffee Creek?"

"She was thorough. A search of death records for the year in question turned up the John Doe who died in that fire on Silver Creek Ranch. When she discovered that the body was roughly the same age and size as the missing McBride kid, she drove down to check it out."

"Hell."

"Yes. You realize, of course, that your aunt's barn is less than an hour's drive from Lewistown—where the watch was pawned. Here's where it gets really interesting." She paused a second. "The watch was sold to the pawn shop the day *after* the boy died."

"How is that possible?"

"It must have been stolen. But less than twenty-four hours had passed between the time he ran away from his home in California and his death in the loft of that barn." Which left a really short window of time when the watch could have been stolen.

B.J. swore softly. "Do you think they'll exhume the body?"

"Shouldn't need to. They ought to have dental records and a DNA sample on file. I've put through some paperwork to see if we've got a match. If we do, I'm guessing a state investigator will be appointed to reopen the investigation."

"I see."

Savannah studied his eyes, looking for more than he'd given her so far. But B.J. didn't say anything further. Finally she'd had it.

"Damn it, B.J. Don't you think it's time you told me what really happened that night?"

Chapter 2

"Why?" B.J. felt sick and angry all at the same time. He'd thought about that vagrant a lot in the passing years. Who was he? What had he been doing in a barn that was so far off the beaten track, most people in Coffee Creek didn't even know it existed?

He'd assumed the guy must be homeless. And that he had no family. It seemed logical, since no one had ever come looking for him.

But if he turned out to be this Travis Mc-Bride, then he had been someone's son. And he'd been missed.

The pain the McBrides must have gone through just didn't bear thinking about.

And now Savannah was on his case. "You

never asked me what happened before. Never wanted to hear my side."

She looked shocked. "That isn't true."

"It is."

She shook her head. "I had to come to the sheriff's office to pick up Hunter. I heard the reports you gave to Sheriff Smith. Your parents were there, too. We got the whole story from both you and Hunter."

Yeah. She'd heard the "official" stories. But she'd never asked him privately about what had happened. He'd expected Savannah, of all people, would understand that he would do what he could to protect her brother. He'd done it for her, because he loved her and knew how much she worried about Hunter.

But that had been a long time ago. They were different people now.

"Right. And what makes you think I have anything to add, eighteen years after the fact?"

Savannah's gaze faltered. She glanced down at her hands, which were clenched in fists on her lap, then back at him. "It was just a hunch."

He shrugged. "I hear you're a good sheriff. You should be proud of that. But you and me—we really don't have anything to talk about. If you want to rehash what happened that night, maybe you should track down your brother."

Savannah watched as B.J. got out of her truck and started walking away. She felt empty inside, drained and tired. It had taken a lot of emotional energy to talk to him again after so many years.

He'd been so closed to her. And mad. She hadn't expected the anger.

She glanced at her reflection in the side mirror. She looked rough. It had been a long week. Some vacation. She'd booked the time off to drive out to Oregon in the hopes of meeting up with her brother.

Besides questioning him about the fire, she'd hoped to reassure herself that he'd cut down on his drinking and was putting aside a portion of his winnings the way she'd advised him to do the last time she'd seen him.

Which had been about six months ago now.

The fact that he hadn't shown up as expected should not have surprised and disappointed her.

Yet it had.

She knew most everyone in the world had given up on her brother. But she couldn't. Maybe it was because they were twins and shared a special bond? But no—she and Hunter had never been especially close. How could they be when she'd always felt more like his mother than his sister?

She shifted in her seat, and now, instead of her own reflection in the mirror, she could see B.J. He had turned around to look at her. For a second their eyes met. Then he shook his head and resumed walking away.

She'd known he was registered at the Wild Rogue, too, when she'd made her plans. Maybe all along it had been him she'd wanted to see…?

"Could I really be that stupid?" She jerked the truck into gear and started to drive. It was a long way back to Coffee Creek and she had only two days of vacation left.

B.J. didn't go for the steak dinner he'd been craving. Instead, he sat in his truck and thought. He had a lot on his mind.

His brother Brock, how much he missed him and what a loss his death had been for the family ranch.

The dead guy in the loft—if Savannah was right, he now had a name and a family that was mourning his death, the way all of them were mourning Brock.

And Savannah.

She'd made him angry tonight, but their conversation had also woken up a longing deep inside him. Something he hadn't felt in a long time.

He didn't understand why, after so many years, she could still make him feel this way.

Another half hour went by before he realized what he needed to do. He hitched his trailer to his truck then wheeled up to a drive-through, where he ordered a burger, fries and a large coffee. While he waited for the food, he left a message for his mother and his sister, letting them know that he'd decided to head back to Coffee Creek.

They'd be surprised, to say the least. He was booked for two more rodeos this month and Coffee Creek was definitely not part of the plan.

But his plan had just changed.

He was going home.

It was time.

Two days later, Savannah pulled into the acreage where she and her family had lived since they'd first moved to Coffee Creek when she was fifteen. It was a run-down, twenty-acre parcel of land with several rusty cars that her father had planned to fix up and sell, as well as an old log home in desperate need of staining and a new roof.

Once, there'd been piles of trash everywhere, too, but over the years she'd carted most of it away, either for recycling or to the dump.

She hadn't had time to do any landscaping, though, and no money, either. For the past few years her paychecks had been divided between the monthly fees for the care home and her sister's college. Thank goodness Regan had qualified for almost a full scholarship or the ends of her paychecks never would have met.

When people asked Savannah about the stress of being a sheriff, she never told them the truth. Her family caused her a hell of a lot more anxiety than her job.

For as long as she could remember, it had been this way.

She parked her SUV and went inside, trying not to notice the cracked lino in the kitchen and the dull walls. A coat of paint would make all the difference.

Maybe that was how she should have spent her week off work. At least then she'd have had something to show for her efforts.

A picture on the fridge showed her mother and father during happier times—Regan was sentimental and liked keeping such things. That was back before children had been on the scene and her father had been gainfully employed at his father's oil and gas company in Dallas.

Drinking and gambling—once only occasional dalliances—had become a way of life for her dad after her grandfather died. He'd quit his oil and gas job, sure he could live off his inheritance for the rest of his life. But by the time they moved to Coffee Creek he'd squandered almost all of his investments. He'd had just enough left to buy this small acreage outside town. The idea had been to open a bed-and-breakfast.

What a laugh.

The endeavor had never gone beyond a few scribbles on a notepad.

While her mother didn't drink or gamble, she had her own way of coping with her husband's foibles and that was by withdrawing into her own little world—a pretty garden and her late-night movies were all Francine Moody ever seemed to care about.

Then when Savannah was sixteen her father passed away from a diseased liver. She'd already been providing most of the care for her brother and sister. But at that point she started taking care of her mother, too.

Savannah popped a frozen pasta entrée into the microwave, then gobbled it down between sips of water. She knew she should head to town and visit her mother.

But she was feeling a pull to a different place, and since there were still several hours left to the long June day, she decided to give in to it.

Rather than get back in her truck, she decided to ride the Harley that Hunter had almost finished fixing up the last time he was home.

She'd taken it to the shop to get it roadworthy, and then bought herself a leather coat and helmet. She'd always wanted a horse—something most of her neighbors took for granted—but horses were expensive to keep and the motorcycle was a close second. She enjoyed taking it out for a spin now and then.

Thirty-five minutes later, she turned the bike off the road onto a dirt boundary access lane that divided Maddie Turner's Silver Creek Ranch from Olive Lambert's Coffee Creek property.

The two sisters had long been estranged—for reasons even B.J. had claimed not to understand.

For about a mile Savannah drove on a track that was almost overgrown until she came to the creek that divided the Lamberts' property from the Turners'.

The barn sat on the Turner side of the boundary, in the middle of nowhere. Once used for branding, it was now listing to one side. Most of the wood was charred from the fire, but the rain from the storm that night had saved it from being completely destroyed.

She nudged her boot under the kickstand, then left her bike parked beside an old ponderosa pine. Wading through grass that was almost waist-high in places, she heard rustling from the willows growing close to the creek.

And then she heard the distinctive sound of a horse snorting. She moved closer to the trees, to make sure.

And there he was—a handsome black gelding, all tacked up for riding and tethered to a tree near the water. "Hey, gorgeous. Where's your owner?"

She scanned one side of the creek then the other, before turning to inspect the barn. Just then a cowboy dressed in faded jeans and a blue shirt stepped out into the sunlight.

"Well, Sheriff. Two times in one week makes for some kind of record, doesn't it?"

She felt her heart give a leap. What the hell was B. J. Lambert doing back in Coffee Creek?

Chapter 3

B.J. had been a rodeo cowboy for almost as many years as he'd spent growing up in Coffee Creek. He'd met a lot of women in those eighteen years. None of them had ever meant to him what Savannah Moody had.

Was it because she'd been his first girl? He'd fallen for her the moment she stepped into the classroom, already beautiful at age fifteen in an unstudied, slightly exotic way that made her stand out from the crowd. Lots of the girls in Coffee Creek were blondes or toffee-colored brunettes, while Savannah's hair was thick, wild and nearly black.

Her eyes, smoky and dark, had a mysterious, watchful quality, and her smooth olive skin and generous, full lips sent a sultry invitation that belied her cautious nature.

Her brother had similar coloring, was also tall and naturally thin, but beyond that, the resemblance ended. Hunter had been cocky, belligerent, on the lookout for trouble. In contrast, Savannah was almost always serious, never one to break a rule or stretch a boundary.

B.J. and Savannah had dated for more than two years, and in all that time she'd never let him do more than hold her hand or kiss her modestly. At parties she'd avoided drinking and smoking, which meant she'd always been the designated driver.

Her high standards had carried over into everything she did—whether it was studying or working at a part-time job, or looking after her baby sister. His friends had teased her at first, but Savannah had remained steadfast and eventually she was accepted and even respected.

He'd wanted to marry her.

And now, looking at her as a grown woman, all those old feelings were surging again.

He'd heard her motorcycle approaching and had been watching her for a while. She looked great in a fitted leather jacket and dark jeans that hugged her long, lean physique. She was almost as tall as he was.

As she walked toward him she pulled off her motorcycle helmet and her thick hair cascaded down her shoulders. He swallowed, fighting an urge to reach out and touch.

"Find anything in there?"

He caught a whiff of a fresh orange-blossom scent as she walked past him on her way to the barn. The big doors had long since fallen to the ground, leaving a gaping opening into the building. The walls sagged to the east, so much so that he felt as if one shove would topple the entire structure.

But it was sturdier than it appeared. It had to have been to have survived this long.

"Funny thing, having a barn in the middle of nowhere."

She'd never been here before today. And until today, he had felt no wish to revisit the place where a man had died. "It was used for branding in the spring," he explained. "Back in the days when the Turners were big into cattle, before my grandfather died."

"When was that?" Savannah asked.

"He had a massive stroke the year before I was born. A day later, he was gone. According to his will, the land was divided between his two daughters. Mom inherited a parcel of good grazing fields that butted up to my dad's property. Maddie Turner was left with the rest, including the house, barn and all the outbuildings."

"Is that when the feud between them started?"

"Their relationship was already rough. But it did get worse then. Mom told Corb that Aunt Maddie didn't let her visit their dad after he had his stroke. Twenty-four hours later he died without her having had a chance to say goodbye."

"That's awful."

"Yeah. If it's true." B.J. knew he was supposed to be on his mother's side, but he couldn't help feeling skeptical.

"After her father's death, didn't Maddie keep raising cattle?"

"She tried. But she soon had to scale down operations. Apparently Maddie doesn't have my mother's head for business and she made one bad decision after another. From what I hear, she only has about fifty head now, as well as a few dogs and some chickens."

"So this barn hasn't been used in a long time."

"No."

Savannah pulled a flashlight out of the

breast pocket of her jacket. "Strange she never had it torn down."

B.J. hung back near the entrance. He'd been wishing he had brought his own flashlight and admired her foresight. She traced the beam along the building's foundation until she came to a corner where the boards were almost entirely black: the obvious starting point of the fire.

"I guess Maddie's had bigger problems to worry about than a falling-down barn in the middle of nowhere. But if you hadn't shown up when you did, I might have rectified her oversight." He pulled a pack of matches out of his pocket.

Savannah's light flashed a line across the ground, ending up at his boots, then his face. "No way. You wouldn't have."

But he could tell she wasn't sure. Fact was, neither was he. Burning down this building once and for all would have solved a lot of problems.

And he wasn't thinking about himself here. Though she would never believe that.

Savannah returned to her investigation, trailing the light over the charred boards that led up from the corner and spread out along both the north and east walls of the barn. A good section of both had been severely burned, though the fire had never reached as high as the loft area above them.

"I wonder if Sheriff Smith had an arson team out here to investigate. There was no mention of it in the file." She examined the blackened boards more closely. "You'd think lightning would strike at the roofline, but it doesn't always happen that way."

"When did you find out a man died here?" Savannah asked him.

"Not until the day after the fire."

"That's what Hunter said, too."

He could see the skepticism in her gaze and he glanced away. He was remembering the morning after the fire, when his father had come into the cattle barn to give him the news about the death.

B.J. had been shocked. And afraid. He'd started to tell his dad the truth then, but Bob Lambert had shaken his head. "Don't talk, son. I've been over this with the sheriff and we've agreed there was no way you or Hunter could have realized that guy was in the loft. Unfortunately, that poor vagrant was in the wrong place at the wrong time."

Later, the medical examiner had confirmed that death had been caused by smoke inhalation. A crazy-high blood alcohol level explained why the unidentified young man hadn't woken when the fire started.

Despite the "official story" there had been rumors. Most of them centered around Hunter Moody, who everyone agreed had always been a shady sort—just like his father.

B.J. couldn't do much about the rumors. But he'd kept his promise to his father and remained mum about that night, never telling anyone that Hunter had been up in the loft and must have seen the vagrant.

He could have put all the blame on Hunter, but he hadn't. He'd protected the other guy out of a sense of responsibility. He should have figured out Hunter was up to something and stopped him.

He'd kept quiet for Savannah's sake. She had enough problems with her family. He hadn't wanted to add another.

"You're still not going to tell me what happened, are you?"

Mind reader. "Better ask your brother."

She made a sound of frustration, then gave up on him and resumed her inspection of the barn. "I'd like to get a look at that loft," she said.

He glanced up. Light was coming through gaps in the wood. "It's probably not safe."

"Just a quick once-over."

"I'll go." He leaned some of his weight on the ladder, which was on the opposite side of the barn from where the fire had started. It didn't feel very solid.

"Let me try it," Savannah said. "I'm lighter."

He gave her a "get serious" look, then, despite his better judgment, put a foot on the second rung. Half expecting the lumber to crack apart under his boot, he took another step, and another.

Anxiously Savannah gripped the bottom of the ladder. "Be careful, B.J."

He grinned. "How many times have I heard you say that?" Glancing down, he thought he could see her smile in return. He was just about at the top now. He reached one hand from the ladder to the floor of the loft, and was about to take the final step up when he heard a loud *crack* and his left foot fell through rotten wood.

"B.J.!"

He grasped desperately with his free hand, managing to secure a two-hand hold on the loft, while the rest of his body swung free as the ladder disintegrated beneath him.

"Hang on, B.J.!"

"Believe me, I am." He grunted as he worked at shifting his body weight up to the loft. "You okay down there?" He hoped she hadn't been struck by any of the falling wood.

"I'm fine. Try swinging your legs. If you get some momentum…"

She'd no sooner said the words than he was putting them into action. And the extra momentum did help. He grunted again, pushed hard and finally was able to drag his body up to the second level.

"Look out. I'm tossing you the flashlight," she called. He heard a thud a few feet to his right.

"Don't stand, in case the wood is rotten up there," Savannah added.

"Roger that." He crawled toward the torch and, once he had it securely in hand, switched on the light and played it against the far wall. Slowly he surveyed the space, but saw nothing except a few bales of moldering hay and a pile of blankets in the far corner.

"Any signs of fire up there?"

He studied the rafters and roof for several minutes before admitting, "No. I can see where the guy died, though. There's still a pile of blankets in the corner."

Savannah hesitated. "I don't imagine there can be any physical evidence worth salvaging at this point. But want to take a closer look?"

He did and was already crawling toward

the corner. When he arrived, he carefully set down the torch, then picked up first one blanket, then the other. He saw nothing, but heard the clink of something metal falling to the wooden surface.

Savannah heard it, too. "What was that?"

He flashed light over the area. Something gold sparkled. "It's some kind of coin. Should I leave it here? Or take it?"

Savannah didn't answer for a long time. Then in a quiet voice she said, "Take it."

He slipped the coin in his pocket. Once he'd satisfied himself that there was nothing else he hadn't noticed, he started crawling toward the bales.

"There are some old hay bales up here. Stand back while I toss them down. They'll probably break apart when they fall, then after you mound up the hay, I'll jump."

"I've been wondering how you were going to get down."

"No problem," he said, mostly out of bravado. He was looking at a fifteen-foot drop and these bales were the small, square kind.

"Okay. I'm out of the way."

"Here they come, then." He heaved one, then the other, over the edge. As he'd predicted, the old twine broke apart on impact and the hay spilled free onto the dirt floor.

Savannah lost no time in piling the hay into the softest landing pad possible. "I wish we had more."

"And I wish that damn ladder hadn't broken," he mumbled. He'd better not break an ankle with this fool maneuver. Hobbling around in a cast wasn't his idea of how to spend the summer months.

He sat down, letting his legs dangle over the open side of the loft. Savannah was standing back, watching.

"This is crazy," she said. "Why don't you wait while I drive to my place? I can be back with a proper steel ladder in under an hour."

He didn't fancy hanging around this loft like a damsel in distress for five more minutes, let alone an hour.

"Incoming," he called out. Then he let the rest of his body follow his feet off the edge of the loft.

B.J. rolled as he hit the hay pile and ended up a few feet from the tips of Savannah's boots.

Her heart had taken a leap of its own when he'd jumped, but she managed to sound cool. "You look good down there."

He levered his body up with his strong

arms, then hopped to his feet. "Don't push your luck, woman."

For a moment he stood his ground, too close for comfort, making her aware of how much stronger and tougher he'd grown in the years since he'd left Coffee Creek.

Of course, she was stronger and tougher, too, but mostly in ways that couldn't be seen.

"You all right?" she asked, trying to switch her focus from her feelings—which were ridiculously fragile right now—to his well-being.

He took a few tentative steps. "Seem to be." He handed her the flashlight, which she hadn't even noticed he was still carrying. Then he dug the coin out of his pocket. "What do you make of this?"

She stepped out of the barn, surprised to see that the sun was almost behind the distant Highwood Mountains to the west. She studied both sides of the coin. It looked brand-new, but was dated more than a century ago. "I've never seen anything like this before. I wonder if it's valuable?"

B.J. had followed her outside and now he looked over her shoulder at the coin. "Seems like an odd thing for a young guy to have dropped out of his pocket."

"Maybe our runaway took more than his father's watch with him."

"It does look like something from a collection. Maybe he planned to pawn it for cash."

"Whoever stole the watch mustn't have known about the coin." She put it in her pocket. Strange this wasn't found during the investigation. After eighteen years exposed to the elements, she was certain no fingerprints could have survived. B.J.'s handling of the coin pretty much guaranteed it. But she'd store the coin in the evidence room at the office, just in case it turned out to be significant.

She glanced back at the barn, then at B.J. She wondered what he was thinking. There had been moments, back there, where it had felt like old times between them.

She'd done a lot of thinking on the long drive home from Oregon. For so many years she'd blamed B.J. for the party, and for Hunter's subsequent downward spiral.

She realized now that she'd been unfair.

B.J. had been good to her brother. He'd taught him to ride, and to wrestle a steer and rope a calf—all skills that Hunter still put to good use on the rodeo circuit. He'd included Hunter in their group of friends, most of whom were responsible kids who worked hard at school and were involved in sporting events in their spare time.

The wildest thing they ever did was gather at the creek bank behind Main Street to drink a few beers on weekend nights.

"That party was Hunter's idea, wasn't it?"

"Kind of late now." B.J. shrugged. "But yeah."

"Why did you lie?"

"Why do you think?" he asked quietly.

Her heart sank. There could be only one answer. "You did it for me."

After she'd picked Hunter up from the sheriff's office, her brother had really laid it on thick about how B.J. had insisted they all take their ATVs out to that barn. According to Hunter, B.J. was the one who'd sourced the hard liquor, as well.

She'd been so upset, she'd refused to take B.J.'s calls. And she'd avoided him at school, too.

Two months later, they'd graduated from high school—and then B.J. and Hunter were both gone.

She put a hand on his arm. "I'm sorry."

"Well. It was probably for the best. We were too young."

Back then, yes. She nodded. "So how long are you home for? Where's the next rodeo?"

"Not sure." B.J. picked up his hat, which he'd left on a rock when he'd gone into the barn earlier. He glanced up at the sky and frowned. "Looks like a storm is blowing in."

"That happened fast." She thought of the other night, eighteen years ago. According to her brother, the big thunderstorm had blown in quickly then, too.

B.J. glanced at her motorbike. "You better get moving before those clouds get here."

"You, too."

Yet they both stood for a few seconds longer, watchful and tentative as good memories and bad battled it out. She'd come out here hoping to convince herself that the story Hunter and B.J. had told all those years ago had been true.

Instead, she was certain that there was more to the story. A lot more. And Travis McBride's family deserved to know what it was.

Chapter 4

It was dark by the time Savannah coasted the bike down her driveway. She was glad to see Regan's car parked next to her SUV. While she didn't begrudge her hardworking sister a little fun, lately she'd been going out a lot after work, and Savannah worried she wasn't getting enough rest.

Regan's summer job at Monahan's Equestrian Center started shortly after dawn and didn't end until six o'clock. The work was physically demanding—primarily cleaning barns, grooming horses and oiling tack. Rolling in at midnight, then getting five hours sleep, just didn't cut it in Savannah's opinion.

She parked her bike in the garage—which

was too crammed with junk to fit a car or truck—then went in the back door.

"Regan? I'm home. Did you check the mail?" She shook her hair free from the confines of her helmet, then hung up her jacket.

"I did. Nothing came," her sister called back. "You're just in time for dinner. And we've got a guest. His name is Murray."

Savannah paused before stepping into the kitchen. Her sister rarely invited girlfriends over, let alone a guy. Could this Murray be the reason she'd been spending so many evenings away from home?

Savannah hoped not. The wrong guy at the wrong time could derail Regan's plans for med school. And her sister had worked too hard to let that happen.

"Smells good in here." She smiled at her sister, before checking out their visitor. He was a nice-looking kid, in his early twenties like Regan, with sandy-colored hair that curled around his ears and at the back of his neck. He looked tanned, as if he spent his days outside.

"It's only chili." Regan lifted a wooden spoon out of the pot on the stove. She had dark hair, too—all three of the Moody siblings did, thanks to their mother's French-Canadian blood. But Regan was shorter than

Savannah, with delicate features and a small, pouty mouth.

"You know I love chili." She felt a pang of guilt for going to check out the Silver Creek barn instead of staying home and making dinner for her sister for a change.

"Hi, I'm Savannah." She offered a hand to Murray, who shook it firmly.

"Murray St. Clair. Nice to meet you. I hope you don't mind me showing up for dinner."

"Murray's been here a lot while you were away." Regan said this matter-of-factly, as if it were no big deal. "He brought over a bottle of wine. Help yourself." She nodded to the open bottle of Malbec on the counter. It was already half-empty.

Wine for a midweek dinner was a rarity in the Moody household, but Savannah decided a glass might be a good idea. She had to be calm and not overreact. Regan was twenty-four now, hardly a kid to be ordered around.

"How was the trip to Oregon, Vanna? Did you see Hunter?"

"He didn't show up."

Her sister gave her a look of commiseration. "So you weren't able to surprise him. How disappointing."

"It was." She took a sip of the robust red. "So—how did you two meet?"

"At Monahan's," Murray said.

"He's an instructor," Regan said in a voice meant to convey the superiority of this position over hers.

"Are you working for the summer, like Regan?"

"No. I'm full-time. I've been with Monahan's since I graduated high school."

"He was a year ahead of me." Regan sampled the chili, then nodded. "It's ready. Want to grab some bowls, Mur?"

Savannah was disconcerted to see that he knew the right cupboard to open. After pulling out three bowls, he went to the cutlery drawer and selected spoons, as well.

Regan ladled chili, added a handful of grated cheese, then passed a bowl to Savannah, before serving Murray, then herself.

Savannah sat at her usual spot and waited until the others had joined her. "You must know Cassidy Lambert. She just started working at Monahan's a few weeks ago."

"I do. She's amazing. But then, Straws only hires the best." Murray's face and ears reddened. "Jeez. That didn't come out right. I didn't mean to be bragging or anything."

"But it's true," Regan was quick to point out. "Straws does hire the best, and that includes you."

When she saw the smile her sister gave Murray, Savannah suddenly realized that a lot had happened during the week she'd been away.

Regan had fallen in love.

And judging by the look in Murray's eyes right now, the feeling was mutual.

"So, Murray, any plans for college in your future?"

He shrugged. "I'm pretty happy where I am."

Savannah shifted uncomfortably. Couldn't Regan see that this romance of hers wasn't a good idea? "I guess you know Regan's planning to go to med school."

"*If* I get accepted." Regan stirred her chili, then shot a glance at Murray. "I've been thinking, Vanna. It's been a long time since I took any sort of break. You know I started work just a few days after my final exams."

"You were lucky to get a job," Savannah pointed out. "Med school is expensive."

"Yes. But I'm tired. And what if I don't get into med school?"

"You wouldn't be tired if you didn't stay out until after midnight every day. And you *will* get into med school. I'm sure of it."

Another look passed between the two friends. *Lovers?* Savannah's stomach felt leaden as she realized it was possible. Why, oh, why had she gone searching for her brother when she should have stayed home looking after the one person who truly mattered in this family?

"Even if I do get in—and say I even qualify for a partial scholarship—we can't afford for me to go. There's no way."

"We'll figure something out."

"Will we? Don't you get tired of everything being such a struggle all the time? We never have any fun. It's all studying and working for the sake of a future that never seems to come."

"We have fun. What about Friday movie nights?"

"A TV movie and popcorn. When I was little, yeah, it was kind of neat. But I want to go places and see things."

Savannah realized suddenly that this wasn't aimless complaining on Regan's part. She had an idea. Maybe even a plan. "What are you really saying here?"

Regan glanced at Murray, then took a deep breath. "We're going on a road trip. We'll camp, so it won't cost much money. We've already spoken to Mr. Monahan, and he's agreed to give us four weeks off."

"Four weeks with no salary?"

"It's a drop in the bucket for what I'd need for med school. But four weeks of traveling could change my life."

"Carpe diem," Murray added—not very helpfully in Savannah's opinion.

Living for the moment was a fine philosophy. But where did it get you in the end? With a medical degree, Regan's future would be set. "There'll be lots of time for traveling once you're a doctor."

"You're so stubborn! When will you accept that this dream is simply out of reach?"

"I told you I'd find the money. And I will."

"You've sacrificed enough for this family. You should be dating, going on exotic vacations and having fun, too. Instead, you spend all your time working, visiting our mother in the care home and worrying about me."

Savannah rested her head in the cradle of her hands. The blood was pounding in her forehead. She could feel it. She could also see her sister's point of view. But what Regan didn't understand was how easily life could come unraveled. Without a solid education, she'd never get a good job, the kind that promised a nice home, security and a respected position in society.

There was no more respectable job than being a doctor. And this wasn't something

Savannah had pushed on her sister. This had been her dream since she was little.

Still, she couldn't just shoot down Regan's travel plans. Maybe a compromise? "How about you go camping for a week, then go back to work?"

"I'm sorry you're against the idea, Vanna. But Murray and I are doing this. We've cleared it with Mr. Monahan, and we're leaving in the morning."

"And there's nothing I can say?" Savannah couldn't believe it. Regan had never defied her before.

"Nothing."

B.J. and Big Black rode up to the home barn at Coffee Creek ranch just as the first star appeared in the evening sky. A rhyme from his childhood popped into B.J.'s head as he looked at it. *Star light, star bright...* some load of crap like that. B.J. didn't waste his time wishing on stars. He wouldn't even know what to ask for if he did.

Savannah's face flashed in his mind and he felt an old yearning that should be dead and buried. He could wish on every star in the summer sky and she'd never be his. It was as simple as that.

B.J. dismounted and led his horse into the

barn, where he cleaned and put away the tack, then gave the gelding a good brush-down.

Earlier he'd said hello to Corb and they'd had a little chat. His younger brother was a typical middle child—easygoing and affable. He'd adjusted to being a father and a husband as if he'd been born to the roles. B.J. admired him for that. Even more, he admired him for being able to work with their mother.

Both Corb and Brock had handled Olive a lot more easily than he ever could. It had always been that way. B.J. remembered railing to his father once about the way the family ostracized Maddie Turner.

"It isn't right, Dad. You walked right by her today and didn't say a word. That isn't the way you taught us to treat people."

His father had looked tired and he'd shaken his head when he'd answered. "You're right, B.J. You weren't raised to treat people that way. But sometimes you have to measure one thing against another. Being loyal to my wife is more important to me in this case than doing the polite thing."

"But Mom gets so stubborn sometimes. Are you sure she's being fair?"

"She isn't the only one who can be stubborn, son. Your mom does a lot for you and she deserves your loyalty. As well as your love and respect."

The conversation had ended there and B.J. had not dared raise the topic again. He knew he'd disappointed his father by even asking those questions.

As tough as he found his mother to understand at times, he did recognize that she'd devoted her life to her family and this ranch. She'd been a fiercely protective and caring mother when they were younger. And she'd worked long hours with the cattle and horses, as well.

And it was thanks to her keen business sense that the ranch had done so well after their father's death and the most recent economic downturn. She'd had the good sense to diversify so that besides running over a thousand head of cattle, they had a booming quarter-horse breeding program, as well.

While their mother oversaw the entire operation, Corb was in charge of the cattle side of the business and, since Brock's death, Jackson had taken over the breeding program. His foster brother had been an invaluable part of the core family for a long time now, yet B.J. sensed he wasn't altogether comfortable with his new role.

Finished with Big Black, B.J. let him out

with the rest of the family's horses. The ones that were used for working with cattle and pleasure riding by the family were kept separated from the more expensive quarter horses. It was a precaution that had paid off big-time last month when an unexpected outbreak of strangles had resulted in the entire ranch being quarantined for a month.

If all the horses had comingled, the infection would have caused far more serious consequences than it had.

As it was, Cassidy had lost her favorite mustang, Finnegan. A loss, B.J. knew, that his soft-hearted sister had felt keenly.

Earlier B.J. had decided that he would sleep in his brother Brock's cabin tonight. A long time ago his father had built three cabins along Cold Coffee Lake, which lay about a quarter mile beyond the main house. The idea had been one house for each son, but B.J. had given up his claim to Jackson.

Corb, his new bride, Laurel, and their baby, Stephanie, lived in the third cabin.

The middle one had been vacant since Brock's death last July. It would be a nice quiet place for him to stay until he sorted out what to do with his life.

B.J. was heading there when he noticed a light on in the office of the home barn. He could think of only one person who would be working on the books at this hour, and it was a person he wanted to see.

Sure enough, he found Jackson on the oak chair behind the desk, frowning at the computer monitor.

"Hey, man. Anyone ever tell you that you work too hard?"

Jackson blinked, then rubbed a hand over his eyes. "Maybe a time or two. How are you doing? I thought you were in Central Point this weekend with your family?" Jackson stood, and shook his hand warmly.

When B.J.'s father had first brought Jackson to the ranch, Jackson had been thirteen and B.J. seventeen. They'd butted heads at first. B.J. had resented the fact that his father was paying attention to this kid—this delinquent—who wasn't even part of the family.

But Jackson had worked hard, kept quiet and stayed out of trouble at school, and B.J. grudgingly came to respect and even like the guy.

Eventually he learned enough about Jackson's past to realize the guy deserved a break. His mom had been in jail herself when Jackson got into trouble with the law. And his father had never been a part of his life.

At seventeen B.J. hadn't been able to imagine life without his dad. Now, five years after losing him to a heart attack, he still felt the loss.

"I was there," he said in answer to Jackson's question. "But I decided to come back early." He shared the family's results with Jackson, but brushed off Jackson's congratulations.

"Just another rodeo trophy, that's all. I was glad Cassidy and Farley did so well, though."

Jackson went to the small fridge in the corner of the room and pulled out a couple of beers. "But I thought you had another rodeo in Washington you were headed to next?"

"Had a change of plan. Plus I figured it was time to check up on the place. Frankly, I was hoping to find you enjoying life a little more than the last time I came home."

"And when was the last time?"

"You know damn well when. Last March, when we were celebrating Corb and Laurel's new baby."

"That was three months ago."

"Yup." He eyed Jackson's face, noting the tired lines around his mouth and eyes. "You had any fun at all since then? Dated any pretty girls?"

Jackson snorted. "No time for that nonsense around here."

"You used to find the time to have fun," B.J. recalled. "Blaming yourself for Brock's death is just about the dumbest thing you've ever done."

"I don't blame myself."

"If you'd look me in the eyes when you said that I might be able to believe you." B.J. took a swallow of his beer and regarded his foster brother thoughtfully. He'd never forget the night before the wedding when they'd been discussing the driving plans. Initially he'd been the one who was going to chauffeur Brock and Corb to the wedding, while Jackson drove Olive in a separate car.

It was Olive who had nixed that plan, insisting that her eldest son should be the one to accompany her into the church.

"If I'd been behind the wheel, it wouldn't have changed a thing. Brock would still be dead. Corb would have hit his head and gone into that coma. It wasn't the driver's fault. It was just bad timing."

Both Savannah and a local rancher who had witnessed the accident had agreed on that point. Why couldn't Jackson take any comfort from that?

"Have you ever thought of seeing a counselor or something? Maybe a professional could help."

As he'd expected, Jackson shook his head at the idea. "Naw. It's not just the guilt that bugs me. It's having been there. And seen it all. I'm the only one, you know. To this day Corb doesn't remember the accident, or even the entire week before it happened."

"He's lucky he doesn't—even if it did almost cost him his relationship with Laurel."

Jackson nodded, closing his eyes and rubbing his forehead. "The worst was those ten minutes before help arrived. It was so quiet, I could hear the birds chirping in the brush. But all around me was blood...."

You couldn't be a rodeo cowboy for eighteen years and not have seen a lot of blood and gore. But the picture Jackson was painting broke B.J.'s heart. He wondered why it had taken him so long to talk to Jackson about this. Or maybe it had taken this long for Jackson to be ready to talk. "It must have been hell."

Again Jackson nodded, his gaze fixed despondently on his boots.

"What can I do to help?"

"What can anyone do? I just go on, getting through each day best as I can." He picked up his beer can, looking at it as if it were something strange that he'd never seen before. "Sometimes I wonder, though...."

"What?"

It wasn't easy to get Jackson to open up and talk about himself. Now that he'd cracked a chip in his foster brother's armor, B.J. had to do his best to keep him talking.

"I just wonder if I shouldn't be moving on."

"Work somewhere else, you mean?" B.J. didn't consider himself a sentimental person, but he had to admit the idea was disconcerting.

"I brought it up to Corb once. He took it like some sort of personal insult. It isn't as if I'm not grateful for what your family did for me. I just can't stand feeling like I'm some sort of fill-in for Brock. Living the life that he was meant to have, instead of doing whatever it was that *I* was intended to do."

"Hell. I'm sure Mom and Corb never meant to make you feel that way when they offered you Brock's job."

"Not Corb, for sure," Jackson agreed.

But maybe Olive? B.J. wouldn't put it past her. He suspected that his mother *did* somehow blame Jackson for Brock's death. Olive had never warmed up to Jackson. Even when everyone else treated him like part of the family, she'd maintained an air of cool distance.

He could see how hard this must be for Jackson to handle in the wake of the accident.

"It hurts me to say this, but if you want to leave, then that's what you should do."

"I'm glad to hear you say that. The perfect opportunity just opened up for me, but there is a catch. I'd need to start right away. And you know it would take a while to find a replacement for me here. And even longer to train him…"

That was all true.

But there was one solution.

It would require a commitment that B.J. wasn't sure he was ready to make. But didn't he owe Jackson this much? Jackson, who had shouldered such a burden for this family all on his own this past year?

"I know someone. And he doesn't need any training."

"Really?" A spark of hope lightened Jackson's dark brown eyes.

"Yup." B.J. nodded. "Me."

Chapter 5

After a fitful night spent worrying about Regan, it was a relief to go to work the next morning. Regan and Murray had taken off on their road trip before Savannah had got out of bed. She'd heard them rustling around in the kitchen, then shutting the back door and starting up Regan's Honda Civic.

She'd considered getting up to say good-bye. But they'd obviously planned on a quick exit with no farewells. And maybe they were right. It might be easier this way.

Regan had left a note on the kitchen table at least.

I love you, Vanna. Try not to worry. We'll drive carefully. See you in four weeks! Xoxo Regan.

So there. It was done.

Not in the mood for breakfast, Savannah dressed for work, then took a to-go mug of coffee in the SUV with her.

And, finally, her mood lifted. She loved everything about being the sheriff of Bitterroot County.

She loved the uniform she wore, she loved her four-by-four SUV that could handle the worst of roads or weather—and in Montana there was plenty of both—and she especially loved her badge.

The population of Bitterroot County was small, less than ten thousand people, and so her office was sized accordingly. She oversaw a staff of three full-time deputies, one part-time officer and a full-time dispatcher. Aside from her dispatcher, Haley McKenzie, everyone on her staff was male and older than she.

A lot of people asked her why a woman would want to work in such a male-dominated world. The choice might seem strange to some, but it was all Savannah had wanted to do since Sheriff Smith had come to the high school to talk at an assembly. She'd been so impressed.

Later, she'd gone up to the man. All the boys had wanted to see his gun. She was impressed by the badge. She'd told him then, bold as could be, "I'm going to be sheriff of Bitterroot County one day."

To his credit, Sheriff Smith had encouraged her. Seven years later, he'd hired her on as a rookie deputy. Ten years after that, when he was ready to retire, he'd supported her campaign to replace him.

No one in her family had been keen about her career choice, though. Before his death, her father had told her, "It's a rough world out there, girl. You'd better be a teacher or nurse. You can always get a good job with training like that."

But every county needed a sheriff, too, and Savannah hadn't been deterred. She'd studied law enforcement at school and gone straight from that to working as a deputy.

Despite her fears that the citizens would see her as too young, the wrong sex or, worse, bring up the disreputable drinking and gambling past of her father, she'd pursued her goal. She still couldn't believe she'd won and gave all the credit to Sheriff Smith's endorsement.

Some people—namely, her mother, brother

and some of the citizens who hadn't supported her election, including Olive Lambert from Coffee Creek Ranch—had suggested she wouldn't last long in the position.

But after almost three years in the role, Savannah loved the job more than ever. And now that it was time to gear up for the next election, she was determined to keep it.

The sheriff's office was located on Church Street in the two-story brick courthouse. Savannah pulled into her parking space at ten minutes to eight. She found the office quiet. Haley wouldn't be in for another hour. In her small office next to the interview room, Savannah checked her email messages and her calendar. Administrative matters kept her busy until her coffee mug was empty and Haley arrived to start her day.

"How was your trip to Central Point?" Haley was in her mid-twenties, and newly engaged to a successful cattle rancher in the neighboring county of Fergus. She was bright, a good worker and was blessed with such a cute smile and sweet, sunny disposition that all the deputies had professed themselves brokenhearted when she announced she was getting married.

"Long."

"Did you see your brother?"

"He was a no-show."

"Really? The bum." Haley had been in the office with her when she was checking the registration listings for the rodeo and she knew the purpose of the weeklong holiday had been to connect with her rambling twin brother.

"In Hunter's defense, he didn't know I was coming." While her twin didn't have a cell phone, she could have sent a message to his Gmail account. She knew he checked that every week or so.

But the truth was, she'd hoped to surprise him.

And her reward was a wasted week—and the return of B. J. Lambert to Coffee Creek. Not that she really believed he was back here because of her. But it was quite the coincidence.

She slammed her desk drawer a little more vigorously than usual.

"Whoa." Haley, who'd been standing in the doorway during their brief conversation, raised her eyebrows. "Somebody needs more caffeine this morning. Shall I go put on a pot?"

"Don't bother on my account. I've already had mine." She lifted her to-go cup. Both she and Haley had agreed that they needed to cut down on their coffee intake, though it was easier said than done. "I just hope Hunter hasn't gotten himself into trouble somewhere."

"He hasn't phoned for bail. That's a good sign."

Savannah laughed, as if Haley was joking. But while her brother's worst misdemeanor since he'd left home to become a rodeo cowboy was a drunk-and-disorderly, Savannah lived in fear that one day it would be worse.

Of course, if that John Doe turned out to be Travis McBride, and the investigation was reopened, maybe worse had already arrived for Hunter.

And for B.J.

Her cheeks burned as she remembered his anger from the previous day. He'd been right. Instead of getting all mad and giving him the silent treatment, she should have talked to him about what had happened all those years ago.

Maybe then he would have opened up to her.

Because he sure wasn't doing that now.

A new message popped into her email, from the coroner's office. She read it with dismay.

How could they have neglected to save the

dental records and DNA sample from their John Doe? It was standard procedure in cases where bodies were unidentified.

Damn. Much as she hated to criticize her predecessor's work, it sure seemed the investigation into this John Doe's death had been shoddy. Why else had they missed the coin that B.J. had found so easily? And not to have collected DNA evidence…

She could guess what would happen next. June Savage would apply to get the body exhumed.

Savannah closed down her email. "I'm going on patrol for a few hours."

On her way to the door Savannah added, "If we get any calls from the state attorney's office, make sure to let me know right away."

"Will do," Haley promised.

The county cemetery was on Grave Street, past Ed and Abby's feed supply and hardware store. A triple row of pine trees had been planted on the north side of the property to divide the cemetery from the rest of the town.

There was a truck parked in the visitor lot when Savannah pulled in. She sighed when she saw it. Just her luck to show up at the same time as B.J. He wasn't in the truck, so he was probably at his family's grave sites on the other side of the hill. For a moment she considered driving away.

This was all her fault for approaching him in the first place. Now she'd brought him back to Coffee Creek and it seemed she was destined to keep running into him until this whole McBride business was put to rest.

She could come back later.

But in the end, she decided to stay. She'd never been one to run from a potentially awkward situation. She wouldn't be much of a sheriff if she had.

The June morning was already warm. A meadowlark was perched on a fence post near the entrance, singing gaily despite the somber surroundings. As Savannah approached, the bird took off for shelter in a nearby grove of aspen.

Packed gravel paths crisscrossed neatly through the cemetery. As she crested a gentle hill, Savannah finally spotted B.J. She guessed he was standing by his brother's grave, though it could have been his father's, as well. They were side by side with just space enough between them for Olive, when her time came. Savannah remembered all this from Brock's funeral. At the time she'd thought of her own father's plot, and how her mother probably would end up buried there one day, too.

But not her. No. Savannah could not imagine resting peacefully beside the parents who had caused her so much grief in life. Her will stated explicitly that she be cremated and her ashes spread out in the mountains somewhere.

B.J. was wearing his hat, and by the angle of the brim, his head was lowered in either prayer or quiet contemplation.

She left him in peace and headed toward her original destination, the grave site of the unknown traveler.

That was how he had been buried, the unfortunate young man who'd had the bad luck to be passed out in the loft of an abandoned barn when it happened to catch on fire.

Happened? No. She couldn't believe it was coincidence that he'd been up there. She now knew just how isolated that barn was. No way would a stranger just "happen" to pass by and take refuge.

She went to look at the gravestone. She'd only ever seen it in passing and had never paid it much attention. Now she took in the simple marker with its two-word engraving.

And she wondered how long it would be

before the orders came for the body to be exhumed.

"So. We meet again."

She hadn't heard B.J.'s footsteps. He must have cut across the grass rather than taken the longer gravel path. He moved up beside her to read the inscription on the headstone.

"The unknown traveler. I always wondered what happened to his body."

"Your father never told you?"

"He didn't volunteer the information and I never asked. Guess we both wanted to put the episode behind us."

"Hunter felt the same way. Wouldn't talk about it, even with me. Not that we talked much after that night."

Keeping Hunter on the right path with his schooling had always been a struggle for Savannah. But he'd begun skipping a lot of classes after the fire. In the end, he hadn't finished the year with enough credits to graduate.

At the time it had felt like the end of the world to her. But over the years she'd learned to let go of her feeling of responsibility for her brother. She wished he'd save more, drink less, maybe even find a nice, grounded woman and settle down.

But those were all Hunter's choices to make.

She let out a long breath, then sneaked another look at B.J. He hadn't shaved that morning, but with his dark hair and firm chin, he only looked more handsome for it.

How many hearts had he broken in the past eighteen years?

"If this truly is Travis McBride, his family is going to have the right to ask some questions about that night. The story about the lightning and him just happening to be passed out in the loft—it won't cut it."

"I know."

She waited, and when he said nothing further, she asked, "Is this still about protecting Hunter?"

He laughed bitterly. "That'd be pretty foolish of me, wouldn't it? Protecting the brother of a girl I haven't dated since high school?"

Foolish? Maybe. But also noble. And so like the boy she remembered.

"I'm sorry I wasn't a better friend to you back then, B.J. I did care about you."

"It would have meant a lot to hear you say that then."

"I know. I wish—" She tried to turn away, but he placed his hands on her shoulders, locking her in place.

"What do you wish?"

She averted her head, disconcerted by the

emotion in his voice and on his face. She had enough training that she could have easily broken away if she wanted to. But she let him continue to hold her at arm's length.

They'd gone so long without having this conversation. She was surprised he'd brought it up now.

"Does my opinion really matter so much? After all these years?"

The sun had been behind a cloud, but then it shifted and brilliant sunshine cut through the trees. B.J.'s face was bathed in the golden light and she could see the green flecks in his dark gray eyes.

"It shouldn't, should it?"

His cryptic comment wasn't an answer. But then, she hadn't answered him, either.

"I thought I could trust you to keep him out of trouble. But I see that was unfair. Expecting too much. He just got worse after that night, B.J. I spent so much time worrying about him and trying to keep him in school and out of trouble, that I just let our relationship slide."

"You always did have too much on your plate." Finally he released his hold, his expression disappointed. "But I needed you, too."

"Back then, it seemed as if Hunter needed me more."

After all, B.J. had had so many advantages over her brother. A stable family life. A father who was a good role model. And a mother who cared what happened to him more than she cared about the flowers growing in her garden.

"You were more of a parent to him than a sister."

It was so true. And it still was. "Can you at least promise me that you and Hunter didn't know he was in the loft when that fire broke out?" Even as she asked the question, she knew it was a mistake, that she was better off not knowing.

Yet she couldn't help waiting anxiously for his answer.

B.J.'s gaze had dropped to his boots. He shifted his weight from one leg to the other before finally lifting his eyes to meet hers. "We didn't know. I promise."

She wished she could believe him.

B.J. hadn't expected coming back to Coffee Creek would be this hard. That spending time with Savannah would be so painful. After so many years he'd figured he might have stopped caring by now.

But he hadn't.

If anything she was more beautiful now that she was older. And the power and authority she'd earned during her years of work as first a deputy, and now sheriff, only added to her attraction.

He'd never liked weak people.

And Savannah was anything but that.

She wasn't stupid, either. She knew he wasn't telling her the truth about that night. But she didn't know, and he hoped she never did, his reasons for being evasive.

After their awkward meeting at the cemetery, B.J. went to grab coffee and a bun from the Cinnamon Stick Café. Though Winnie Hays had opened it only a few years ago, it had quickly become a favorite meeting spot for many of the local residents, specially famous for the cinnamon buns baked by former bronco rider—and recovered alcoholic—Vince Butterfield.

B.J. was prepared to join a queue for service, but the café was atypically quiet when he stepped inside. He nodded hello to Tabitha Snow, the local librarian, who was on her way out.

"B.J.….nice to see you. Having a good season?"

"Good to see you, too, Ms. Snow. And not

bad, thanks," he added, in response to her question about his rodeo standings. He held the door wide until she'd passed through, then entered the now empty, deliciously scented space.

Dawn Dolan, a cute little thing with a blond ponytail and a smattering of freckles on her nose, gave him the sort of smile he usually shied away from with girls as young as she was.

But he needed his breakfast, damn it.

"Hey, Dawn. Mind pouring me a coffee and getting me one of Vince's buns to go?"

"No problem, B.J. How did you do at the Wild Rogue?"

"Best all-around," he admitted, "but Cass took third in barrel racing and Farley came in first in steer wrestling." He glanced behind her, toward the kitchen. "Is Laurel in today?"

He wanted to ask if she and Corb could make it to the big house for dinner tonight. Much as he dreaded such gatherings, it was time for a family meeting.

"She and Stephanie don't usually come in until around ten." She glanced at her watch. "That's in just thirty minutes. You could sit and wait if you wanted."

"No, thanks. I'll just send Corb a text message." He pulled out his phone to do it before he forgot. "Might as well say hi to Vince, then I'll be on my way. Mind if I step through to the kitchen?"

"No need. Heard your voice, just had to punch down the dough before I came out to see your ugly face." Vince, dressed in the odd combination of Western jeans, boots and a snowy-white baker's apron, came out of the kitchen with a rare smile on his face. Long days in the sun, too much partying and not enough sleep had all taken their toll on Vince—he looked every day of his sixty-odd years and then some.

Vince was a man of few words and carefully guarded emotions. But he'd been on the circuit and he loved catching up on the news whenever B.J. was in town.

The two chatted while Dawn rang in his sale then poured his coffee and packaged his cinnamon bun.

"So where's the next rodeo?" Vince asked.

"Not sure. I'm planning to hang out at home for a while."

"Yeah?" Vince looked surprised, but didn't probe. Then he startled B.J. by adding, "That's probably a good idea."

B.J. hesitated. Vince wasn't normally one to offer opinions or advice. "Any particular reason you say that?"

"If I said it, I guess there was a reason."

Hard to argue with that. But obviously Vince wasn't in the mood to elaborate. He rarely was.

"Okay, then. See you around, Vince."

The retired cowboy nodded before returning to his kitchen.

Next stop was Molly's Market to pick up groceries for that evening's dinner—which he planned to cook. As he selected a cut of beef for fajitas, B.J. ruminated over Vince's comments. Clearly Vince felt B.J. was needed here in Coffee Creek. Was it possible the old bronco rider had heard that the case of the unknown traveler was about to be reopened? Or had he been referring to something else entirely? Something a little closer to home?

Olive, Cassidy and Farley arrived back at the ranch that afternoon at five, tired from their long drive, but still jubilant over their wins at the rodeo. B.J. had already put the beef to marinate and chopped up plates of peppers and onions. He met his family at the front door, along with Sky. Cassidy's fourteen-year-old border collie usually hung out at one of the cabins by the lake, but she seemed to have a sixth sense when it came to anticipating Cassidy's arrival at the big house.

Cassidy rewarded her with a hug, while she gave her older brother a smile and a curious look.

"So you're really here." Olive slipped out of the driver's seat of her SUV—his mother was incongruously petite in comparison to the sturdy all-wheel-drive vehicle. "Your note caught us by surprise. I thought you were driving up to Washington next?"

"I've had a change of plans and I was hoping I could run them by the family tonight after dinner." B.J. gave his mother a kiss, hugged his sister, then clapped a hand on Farley's shoulder. "Can you and Cassidy make it? I'm cooking."

"You are?" his mother asked, her raised eyebrows belying the mild tone of her question.

"There's a first time for everything. Hope you don't mind me taking over the kitchen?" He knew she wouldn't. Cooking wasn't one of his mother's favorite activities. Most of the big-house meals were prepared by the housekeeper. Currently this was Bonny Platter, a good-natured, no-guff woman in her fifties who had moved to Coffee Creek three years ago and been glad to find a steady, well-paying job. B.J. had sent her home early an hour ago, assuring her that she deserved the break.

B.J. could only imagine the challenges involved in working in his mother's household. Olive was hard enough to please when it came to the barns, let alone the house.

"I have no objection to you cooking, B.J. Whenever you are so inclined, please feel free."

He grinned. "I thought you'd say that. By the way, I've already invited Corb, Laurel and the baby."

His mother's face lit up, until he added, "And Jackson, too, of course."

"Of course," she added, drily.

"We can start with margaritas on the back deck. I have a pitcher ready to go in the fridge."

Cassidy gave him a glowing smile. "Then what are we doing out here? I'll grab the pitcher if you get the glasses, Mom."

Corb, Laurel and baby Stephanie joined them about thirty minutes later. B.J. hadn't spent much time with babies, but he got a kick out of holding his new niece and trying to coax smiles and giggles out of her. They kept the conversation light. No sense getting down to business until Jackson showed up.

Their foster brother didn't arrive, however, until minutes before the fajitas were served.

B.J. had barbecued the steak, then sliced it thinly and served it alongside bowls of guacamole, shredded lettuce and the sautéed onions and peppers. A stack of warmed corn tortillas and a bowl of salsa completed the meal.

They ate outdoors, enjoying the warm early-summer evening. Whether it was the plentiful food, the good weather or the two pitchers of margaritas that had been savored over the course of the evening, the overall mood was congenial and relaxed when B.J. deemed the timing right to make his announcement.

He raised his eyebrows at Jackson, who knew what he was planning to say, then got up from his chair in order to silence the conversation.

Cassidy and Farley, who'd been replaying the details of the rodeo for Corb and Laurel's benefit, both fell silent.

"You have something to say, bro?" Corb asked.

"I do." With the attention on him, B.J. sat down again. "Jackson and I both have announcements to make."

Olive's keen eyes shifted from her son to Jackson, then back again. "What's this about, B.J.?"

"It's about the ranch," he said. "Jackson has

had an offer for another job and he wants to take it. And I'm prepared to handle his responsibilities here—if that's okay with you and Corb."

The light that exploded in Olive's expressive green eyes was nothing less than jubilant. He knew he'd just granted two of her deepest desires in one shot.

But Corb's reaction was more ambivalent. "B.J., that's awesome—you know we'd love to have you back here working full-time. But Jackson doesn't have to leave. God knows, there's enough work—and responsibility— for both of you."

"I do appreciate that," Jackson said slowly. Then he turned to Olive. "I truly am thankful for everything the Lambert family has done for me since I was thirteen. I've been feeling for some time, though, that I ought to be moving on."

"I'm sure a man of your talents has plenty of opportunities," Olive said.

Corb looked at his mother as if she were crazy. "His opportunities are here at Coffee Creek Ranch." He tossed his napkin on the table. "I thought we already settled this, Jackson."

"You told me the family needed me, and so I agreed to stay," Jackson countered. "But now B.J. is willing to step in. I figure that frees me to make my own choices."

"Hell. I never wanted you to stay on out of obligation." Corb's voice betrayed his hurt. "You're like family to me. To all of us. I thought we were the same to you."

Laurel put a hand on her husband's shoulder, as if sensing his pain and wanting to show her solidarity.

"I'm not doing this to hurt you or your family," Jackson insisted.

Corb's expression told him, however, that he was doing exactly that. Finally Corb refocused his attention to his older brother. "Well. You two obviously have this all worked out."

"We just spoke yesterday," B.J. said, not wanting Corb to feel as if there'd been some sort of conspiracy between him and Jackson.

"Wow. These are pretty big decisions to be making in one day." Corb folded his arms across his chest, as if he could block out their words if he just tried hard enough.

"Agreed. But Jackson has been offered a job. And I believe they want him to start right away." B.J. glanced at Jackson for confirmation.

Jackson nodded.

"Well." Olive's voice was crisp and decisive. "It doesn't sound like any decisions are needed on our part. I'm delighted to hear that B.J. will be stepping in to his rightful place on this ranch."

Yet again, B.J. endured her triumphant smile.

"And I think we should all be encouraging Jackson to take this new opportunity," Olive continued. "He's thirty now, and I'm not surprised he wants to move on with his life."

B.J. didn't bother pointing out his mother's hypocrisy. She certainly had never felt that he, Corb or Cassidy needed to "move on with their lives." In fact, she'd fought tooth and nail against it.

Then again, they all knew she'd never accepted Jackson as part of the family, despite Bob Lambert's efforts.

"Since I can't seem to get you to change your mind," Corb finally conceded, "all I can say is I hope it's a really good job that you're leaving us for."

"Where *will* you be working?" Cassidy asked, finally saying outright what they'd all been wondering.

"I won't be going far. In fact, we'll still be neighbors."

B.J. couldn't think what he meant. Farley's land abutted theirs to the north, while the county road bordered the south and east property lines. Was Jackson talking beyond the road?

But Cassidy figured out the answer first. "You're going to Silver Creek Ranch?"

Everyone turned to Jackson. It seemed even the birds fell silent waiting for his answer.

When he nodded, Olive's face turned sickly pale. Her lips thinned and her eyes narrowed sharply as she fixed her gaze on the man her husband had treated like one of his sons. "You'd do that to us? After all we—and especially Bob—did for you?"

Jackson let out a long, tired breath. "I was hoping you wouldn't see it that way."

With a quavering voice Olive asked, "How else *should* I see it?" Slowly she rose to her feet. "I'm just glad Bob didn't live to see this day." Deliberately she folded her napkin, placed it on the table and headed into the house.

B.J. knew she expected at least one of them to follow her, commiserate on Jackson's betrayal and condemn his evil actions. But they were all too curious to hear the rest of the story.

"How did this come about?" Cassidy shifted her chair closer to Jackson's.

"You all know that since Brock passed on, I've been helping Maddie out with the odd job."

"That's an understatement," Farley said. "You put a new roof on her house and the cattle barn."

"Yeah. Working in dribs and drabs. But the place is in bigger trouble than that. She's sold off most of her livestock and run up some loans. And then she found out she had lung cancer."

"How is she doing?" Cassidy asked.

"She's out of the hospital for now, but she's refused treatment, and I don't think she'll have long. Maybe six months to a year."

Jackson's blunt prognosis hit B.J. hard. This woman was his aunt. Too late, he realized that whatever the reason behind the family differences, he never should have let the feud carry on this long.

"Is she planning to go to a hospice?" Laurel asked, concerned.

"No. She wants to die at home."

Jackson sure wasn't sugarcoating any of this.

"The agreement we've come to," Jackson continued, "is that I'll board with her so she isn't alone. As well, I'll take over operation of the cattle business—such as it is."

"I do feel badly for her," Corb said. "It was

real nice of her to remember Brock with all those flower wreaths, and I'm sure she's a decent lady despite what Mom would have us believe. But this doesn't sound like much of an opportunity for you."

"You haven't heard the whole deal," Jackson said. "In return for my labor and the investment of all the capital I've saved up over the years, Maddie Turner is planning to bequeath her ranch to me."

Chapter 6

"Heck and darn!" Cassidy exploded with an expression that B.J. had always found mildly annoying. "She's giving you the whole five hundred acres?"

Jackson shrugged. "I tried to talk her out of it. I told her that she should divide the land up among the three of you—her blood relations."

B.J. shook his head. "We don't deserve it." What had any of them done for their aunt Maddie? Nothing. It was only Brock—with his kind heart and willingness to rebel against their mother's wishes—who had bothered to get to know the aunt who had lived in such close proximity to them all these years.

"That's not why she's doing this," Jackson

insisted. "She doesn't blame any of you for the past. She says there are other reasons she wants me to have the land. Reasons that will become clear in time." He shook his head. "I know, it sounds damn mysterious."

"Maybe she's losing her marbles?" Corb ventured.

"Not Maddie Turner." Farley's tone was firm. "I've been her vet for as long as I've been practicing, and I assure you that woman is as sharp as they come. Though I do believe she was too kindhearted to succeed in the beef business."

"Can you come up with a rational explanation for what she's doing, then?" Jackson said. "Because I sure as hell can't."

"You could always say no," Corb pointed out.

"And have her spend her last months alone and impoverished? I don't have a fortune saved up, but it's enough to make sure she has groceries and a warm house for her final days. Even so, I'm going to have to sell some of the land in order to build up the herd." Jackson glanced at Corb. "You interested in buying?"

"I'm not sure how Mom would feel about that."

"Well, if Olive doesn't want the land, then

I've got another buyer in mind. A guy by the name of Sam O'Neil has been purchasing property in the Coffee Creek area lately, including the tract on the other side of Silver Creek. I'm sure he'd be glad to snap up another hundred acres."

B.J. put up a hand to stop Corb from answering. As the oldest, he felt that he should have some say in this, too. "I vote we don't upset Mom with this. It's such a small parcel of land. If you've got a buyer lined up, then go ahead and sell it."

He took a deep breath. "And if Maddie wants to leave you her land, then that's her business. Agreed?"

He turned from Corb to Cassidy, and they both nodded.

"But the news about Maddie's health— that's something else. When we were kids it made sense for us to respect our parents' wishes as far as our relationship with our aunt was concerned. But we're adults now. It's time all of us considered our past actions and whether they were right or wrong. If we want to make amends, sounds like we'd better do it soon."

The next afternoon, after a long day of reacquainting himself with the business end of the quarter-horse breeding operation, B.J. got in his truck, intending to drive over to Silver Creek Ranch and introduce himself to his aunt. His only hesitation was his fear of having his actions misinterpreted. He didn't want Maddie thinking he was making a last-ditch play for a share of her inheritance.

As he was mulling all of this over in his mind, he ended up driving in a completely different direction than he'd planned. It was five-thirty when he pulled up to Savannah Moody's acreage.

The place was a mess. It always had been.

The house—a prefab log structure in need of staining—had been situated in an unattractive hollow, surrounded by a scramble of brush and the occasional ponderosa pine. About two hundred yards from the house, a couple of abandoned old cars were rusting out in the open. Once, there'd been a junk heap next to the cars, as well. That, at least, had been cleared away in the past few years.

Savannah's SUV was parked by the side of the house, so he knew she was home. He didn't realize she was outside, though, until he almost stumbled over her. She was on the other side of a clump of overgrown lilacs, her back to him as she crouched beside a neatly tended perennial garden, pulling out weeds.

He was taken aback by how sexy she looked in a simple pair of shorts and a tank top, her long hair tied in a loose ponytail.

He stopped the moment he spotted her, considering how to let her know he was here without startling her.

He should have known better.

"Next time call first, okay?" She stood up, brushed the dirt from her knees and only then turned to face him. She was frowning.

Even her frown was sexy. How did she do that?

"So you agree there should be a next time." He hadn't intended to flirt with her. But that's how his comment came out.

"Only if you have a good reason. As the county sheriff, it's my job to be available to any citizen who needs me."

He wondered what she'd say if he told her he needed her, all right. Real bad. But he decided not to push his luck. Trying not to ogle her legs, he shifted his gaze to the flowers, many of which were in full spring bloom. "This is nice. You'd never guess it was here from the road."

"Mom's private little piece of heaven. I went to visit her after work today. Did she ask how I was doing or about Hunter or Regan?

Oh, no. But she did make me promise that I'd weed her perennial bed for her."

"Parents. Can't live with them. Can't get born without them."

She almost smiled. "Sometimes, I swear, my mother makes a test tube look warm and caring."

He had moments like that with his own mother, so he could relate. But Savannah was already shaking her head.

"Did I just say that? It's been a bad week...." She picked up a bucket full of weeds and started carrying it farther up the hill that rose beyond the house and what passed as a front yard.

Since she hadn't booted him off her land, and he liked being around her, B.J. followed. As they crested the hill he took in an amazing view of mountains and forest, with a sparkling creek running through the foreground.

"Hell. I forgot how pretty it is up here."

When they were younger, he'd spent a fair amount of time on the Moodys' land, hanging out with Savannah and Hunter. He'd been so crazy about her at that time that he'd even been willing to do her chores, just for the chance to be near her. Since she'd had almost full responsibility for her younger sister, he'd embraced that role, too, becoming a surrogate older brother to the little munchkin.

"Is Regan home?"

"No."

The answer was curt and he wondered if something was wrong. Savannah shifted the pail from one hand to the other. He wanted to offer to carry it for her, but knew she'd snap at him if he did.

"It is a million-dollar view," she finally said, "or at least four hundred thousand." She went to a compost heap tucked behind a grove of aspen and dumped out the weeds.

"Why do you say that?"

"Four hundred thou?"

He nodded.

"'Cause that's what I've been offered. Someone by the name of Sam O'Neil."

He'd heard that name just yesterday. "Sounds like the same guy who wants to buy a piece of Silver Creek Ranch." He imagined an aerial view of the region. At least two midsize ranches lay between the far border of his aunt's property and Savannah's place. Was this O'Neil buying up random parcels of land? Or planning to piece them together, eventually?

If so, he had to have mighty deep pockets.

"Are you seriously considering selling?"

He'd been raised to believe that land and family were one and the same. Preserving the past meant securing the future. You might as well consider selling a child as a portion of your land.

"If Regan gets accepted to med school—yes."

He saw determination in the set of her jaw. But there was a note of desperation in her voice that he suspected she hadn't intended for him to hear. "Where will you live?"

"I guess I'll rent a place in town."

He waved a hand at the view. "You wouldn't miss all this?"

"I would and I wouldn't. It's a beautiful parcel of land, but my family has never made much of it. In some ways living here is a constant reminder of all of our failures."

She started walking down the hill toward the creek, and again he followed, admiring her long-legged stride and the graceful way her feet, in a tattered pair of sneakers, found purchase on the uneven ground.

She stopped to point out footings for a home that had never been built. "That was supposed to be the bed-and-breakfast."

"What happened? Did your dad lose interest in the project?"

"Probably. Or maybe he couldn't put together the financing. He was always having grand ideas—usually between gambling and drinking binges. Those old cars out front? He and Hunter were going to fix them up and sell them for fortunes. Now they're eyesores. One day I'll have to hire a tow truck and have them hauled to the dump. And over there?"

She pointed to a field so overgrown you could hardly tell it had once been tilled.

"That was going to be the vineyard." Again, she shook her head. "In the heart of cattle country. Can you imagine?"

It was his turn to shake his head. But what he really wanted was to wrap his arms around her waist and feel her lean back against him, the way she once had.

Abruptly she turned away from the field. "Why did you come here tonight?"

"I left home heading someplace completely different. Ended up here." He stared into her eyes, wondering if she still felt anything for him. Yes, it had been a long time. But his attraction to her—sexual, but far more than that—was stronger than ever.

"What do you want?" Her voice was quiet, but edged with desperation.

"What I always wanted." He took a step forward and reached for her chin. He couldn't let her look away from him. He needed to see the dark pools of her eyes and hope that some hint of her true feelings would be revealed. "You."

B.J. was messing with her. Big-time. It wasn't fair that he could do it so easily. One touch from his fingers. A simple word spoken so quietly. *You.*

Her body had turned to fire when he said that. She'd longed to reach for him, or even take a single step in his direction. She could tell that was all that he was waiting for. One little sign.

But did he really want her? And in what way? She'd heard how the available women in Coffee Creek talked about him when he was home. How sexy he was, how strong and handsome. The general consensus was, if B. J. Lambert crooked his finger, they'd come running. It was probably like that for him everywhere he traveled. And he traveled to a lot of places.

"Why me? I'm sure you have your pick of women."

"There's no one serious in my life. Hasn't been for—" He hesitated a beat. "A long time."

He looked at her steadily. Intently. She remembered a time when she would have been certain it meant that he was telling the truth.

"I'm just the girl that wouldn't sleep with you. That's what you want, isn't it? Another notch on your belt?"

"My belt has plenty of notches. More than I need." He shoved his hands in his pockets and narrowed his eyes. "You don't trust anyone, do you?"

"Professionally—no." Objectivity was important when you worked for the law. Listen to what people have to say. But trust the evidence. Facts never lie.

"What about privately?"

She thought about the people in her life. Once, she would have said that she trusted Regan. But since her sister had taken off on her road trip with Murray, she was no longer certain.

"I don't see the distinction. I know a lot of people in this county. But when you're the sheriff, you're treated differently." It had been the same when she was a deputy, too. Even with the law-abiding friends she'd grown up and gone to school with, there was now a fine line that precluded true intimacy and trust.

"Can I take that to mean there isn't a man in your life?"

"That's none of your business." She picked

up the pail she'd been carrying earlier, needing some sort of barrier between them. "It's time for my dinner. You'd better hit the road."

"You're not going to invite me in?" His voice was gently mocking.

"For what? A frozen entrée heated in the microwave? I'm sure you can do better."

"Maybe I can. And so can you. If you invite me in, I'll cook you something."

Savannah was appalled by how badly she wanted to say yes. She hadn't realized until that moment how lonely she felt.

Regan's betrayal—and that was how she saw it, no matter how unfair it sounded—had been the last, unbearable loss.

But turning to B.J. for comfort wasn't the solution. At least not until this Travis McBride situation was resolved. But by then he'd probably have left town for his next rodeo.

"I don't have much in the fridge, just eggs, milk and bread. If you're hungry, you'd do better to drive into town." She started back toward the house, trying not to feel embarrassed by the peeling paint and the torn screen on the back door. She was just reaching for the handle to let herself in, when she heard the sound of a truck.

B.J. had moved up the side of the house,

where he had a view of the road. "Looks like you have another visitor."

She sighed. "Must be my lucky day."

B.J. stayed a step behind Savannah as she changed courses and went around the house. She hesitated for a moment when she saw the vehicle—a forest-green Jeep with the top down. Inside was a woman with brown hair, cut to her chin, wearing sunglasses and talking on her cell phone.

As he and Savannah moved closer, she terminated the call.

"I've got to go. I'll be in touch later." She put down the phone and climbed out from the driver's seat, offering Savannah her hand even before she was close enough for Savannah to shake it.

The woman was in her late forties, B.J. guessed. While her clothing was practical—jeans and a tailored blouse—her makeup, and expensively understated jewelry, gave her a well-groomed appearance.

"Sheriff Moody. Good to see you again."

He didn't think Savannah returned the sentiment. She just nodded.

The woman slid her glasses up to rest on the top of her head. Her eyes, wide and thickly lashed, gave him a quick study. Before she had a chance to say a word, he introduced himself.

"B. J. Lambert. I take it you're the investigator from L.A.—June Savage." He didn't word it as a question, because it wasn't. He'd seen her Californian plates, and Savannah's wary reaction had told him the rest.

"I am. And how convenient to find you here. You were with Hunter Moody when that barn 'caught' on fire, weren't you?" Her eyebrows, as well as the tone of her voice, made it clear that she wasn't buying the official version of events.

She turned to Savannah. "Can we go inside to talk?"

He could sense Savannah's reluctance, even before she replied, "You should have made an appointment to speak with me at my office. But there are some chairs on the front porch, and I guess I can spare you a few minutes now."

The porch was actually the one place on the property that looked inviting. The wooden boards had been stained a mossy-green and there were four wicker chairs with plump cushions sitting in a line next to a big urn of colorful flowers.

Savannah didn't offer refreshments—not so much as a glass of water—and when it came time to sit on one of the chairs, she perched herself on the very edge.

"I don't want to waste your time." June's eyes were doing a lot of dancing between B.J. and Savannah. He could tell she was trying to assess their relationship. Good luck to her with that one. He didn't have a clue where he really stood with Savannah himself.

Her words had been very clear. She had no time for him.

But her eyes had been sending a different message entirely.

At some point he was going to have to sort out the mixed signals and convince her that he was back in Coffee Creek to stay and she could trust him again. But right now, he'd better focus all his attention on the lady from L.A. She was sharp, he guessed, and he didn't want to underestimate the danger that she posed.

All he needed now was for Hunter to end up in trouble again. Nothing would get Savannah more riled than that.

"I just got back from having a look at the barn on Silver Creek land."

"I hope you had permission from the owner," Savannah said quickly.

"Sure did. Lovely lady, Maddie Turner,

though she didn't seem to be feeling very well."

B.J. felt a jab from his conscience at this. No getting sidetracked tomorrow. Right after his morning chores he was paying his aunt that visit.

"Miss Turner said they haven't used the barn since the incident," June elaborated, "and I was welcome to poke around—as long as I was careful that I didn't hurt myself since she doesn't have insurance."

B.J. immediately thought of the broken ladder. He glanced at Savannah and could tell that she was thinking the same thing.

June's eyes narrowed and B.J. realized she was following the silent interplay between them. "I was surprised to see how far it was from the main road."

Damn. She was even sharper than he'd thought.

"Makes a person wonder how a boy from L.A. could have found his way there. He certainly couldn't see it from the road."

"I wasn't the sheriff at the time, obviously, but yesterday I took a look at that barn myself," Savannah said calmly. "And I wondered the same thing."

"Must have been some local boys who took him out there to rob him."

"We have no evidence to support that."

"What about the watch?"

"That could have been stolen earlier. Before he ended up in the barn," Savannah pointed out reasonably.

"Possible," June Savage conceded. "But not likely."

June looked straight at him then, and B.J. felt an overwhelming wave of guilt. Suddenly he wanted, desperately, to tell both these women the complete truth about that night.

If it was his own reputation on the line, he would have.

But how could he condemn Savannah's brother? To this day he didn't understand Hunter's motives for what he'd done. Wild as the boy had been back then, he couldn't believe Hunter had purposefully intended that man to die.

So, with great effort, he kept his mouth shut.

"Well," June said. "First things first, I guess." She glanced at Savannah. "I've asked to have the body exhumed. We need to make sure that boy really is Travis. Once the paperwork comes through, I guess we'll start getting some answers."

"Yes, we will, Ms. Savage," Savannah replied with determination. Her words were for the investigator. But she was looking at B.J. as she said them.

Chapter 7

As she watched June Savage drive off in her perky green Jeep, Savannah felt as if every cell in her body was stretched to the snapping point.

"You've got to admire that woman's persistence," B.J. said. "Imagine finding a watch on eBay eighteen years after it had gone missing?"

"She's determined, all right. And I do hope she gets some answers that will bring closure to the McBride family. But there's so much I don't think we can ever know. Like what that kid was doing in that barn in the first place."

"Hardly anyone besides the Lamberts and Turners even knew the barn existed."

Did he realize how damning that sounded? "There must have been someone else who knew, B.J. Unless he accidentally stumbled across the place."

"Impossible." B.J. considered the problem. "I suppose some of the hired men who worked on our family ranches years ago might know about the barn. Plus some of our friends. We often head that way when we go on trail rides."

"Something else that's puzzling me," Savannah added. "According to the M.E.'s report, the unknown traveler had a blood-alcohol-concentration level of almost .2 percent. But no empty bottles were found with his body."

"The sheriff and his men probably removed the bottles," B.J. said.

"There was no mention of that in the report...."

But then, a lot of things were missing from Sheriff Smith's report. She could tell B.J. was thinking the same thing.

"Maybe we should have a chat with our old sheriff tomorrow," he suggested.

While the idea of bothering her former mentor—now retired on a hobby farm outside of Lewistown with his wife and an assortment of pet animals—was unappealing, she had come to the same conclusion herself.

But there was one part of his sentence she had to object to. "*We?* Last time I checked you weren't on the sheriff's office payroll."

"I'm volunteering my services as a concerned citizen."

"How civic-minded of you." She wished he would stop smiling at her. He was acting like the old B.J., as if they were friends, when the very opposite was true. "But totally unnecessary. I can handle the job myself."

"If that's the case, you shouldn't have tracked me down in Central Point."

She'd figured that out already. "That was a mistake."

"Maybe so. But I'm here now. And we can either drive to visit the Smiths together, or I'll follow right behind you. Which do you prefer?"

She shook her head. "Neither. I'm going alone."

"Sorry, sweetheart. You don't have that option anymore."

The way he was looking at her, it was easy to read much more into his words. As if he wasn't just talking about the case, but her life, as well.

Her hands started to perspire.

His claim on her was a very old one. She couldn't afford to let him draw her in again. She wanted respectability and security. Nothing a rodeo cowboy like B.J. had to offer.

Plus it wouldn't look right to the people of this county if she took up with him now, just as new questions had been raised about that old arson case.

The citizens of this town had a right to expect their sheriff to stay impartial.

"You're used to getting your way," she said, struggling to keep her voice dispassionate. "In the rodeo arena and in life." It was part of the package that came with being the oldest son of the largest, most successful ranching family in the county.

"But *I* am the legally elected sheriff in this county," she continued. "And you are not going to tell me how I conduct my business."

Damn B.J. He was looking amused now instead of chastened.

"I'm serious, B.J. You are *not* coming with me tomorrow, or any other day. I strongly suggest you stick to your job and leave me to mine."

"My job, huh?" He crossed his arms and tipped his head to one side. "And what would that be?"

"Rodeos." The sooner he got out of town, the better. "Where's the next one?"

"Actually, there's been a change of plans in my family."

A cold feeling snaked up Savannah's spine. "Oh?"

"Jackson's taking a job with Maddie Turner. And, thanks to nepotism, I'm the new manager of the quarter-horse breeding business."

"You can't be serious." She rubbed her hands on the sides of her hips. B.J. living full-time in Coffee Creek again? It was more than she could handle.

"Oh, but I am," he assured her. "About a lot of things. And one of them is you."

She had no words. Somehow the balance of power had shifted between them. He'd gone from being on the defensive to acting as though he was in charge. She had no idea how it had happened, either. Putting her hands on her hips, she was preparing to order him off her property when he did another totally surprising thing.

He kissed her.

Later, she wondered why she hadn't resisted, pushed him away.

Instead, she'd returned the kiss as if he were the only thing that mattered in her world.

All her responsibilities—as the sheriff, and as a daughter and a sister—all of these were shed like a useless jacket on a hot summer day. For a glorious moment she was nothing but a woman, in an insulated bubble of pleasure.

Eventually the voice of reason grew loud enough for her to hear.

What the hell are you doing?

Finally, she stepped back, the way she should have done in the beginning. "Stop it, B.J."

"Stop what? Wanting you?"

His eyes were so dark with desire and need, she had to glance away. "Yes," she whispered. "Those days are over for us."

"Maybe you think they are—even wish they are," he said. "But eighteen years hasn't changed a thing for me."

B.J. didn't sleep much that night. He kept thinking about kissing Savannah and how great it had felt. Even though she'd only let her guard down for a minute, it had been enough for him to know that she was still the one.

He'd spent eighteen years searching for a replacement for her, only to come home and realize it had always been Savannah and always would be.

The epiphany was exhilarating—and terrifying. Savannah had feelings for him—he was sure of that. But earning her trust again was going to be damn hard. In fact, he couldn't see any way to do it that wouldn't cause her pain. Because clearing his name regarding that vagrant's death meant pointing the finger at her brother.

And he couldn't do that to her.

But that didn't mean he was giving up on the two of them.

B.J. didn't believe in defeat.

"Try again, son" had been one of his father's favorite sayings. And he thought of those words the next morning, after chores, as he headed into town and made a few phone calls.

Savannah had been pretty clear last night. She wanted him to keep his distance. But every instinct he had warned him to do the opposite. He needed to keep as close as possible.

And that included following her today. He had an idea of how Savannah's mind worked, and he intended to take advantage of that.

Savannah woke up feeling uncharacteristically muddled. She sat at the kitchen table for a long time with her coffee, instead of taking it with her to work, as usual. On the table were her notebook and also the slim file she'd found on the John Doe accidental-death investigation.

But she wasn't thinking about work right now.

She'd had the strangest dreams last night.

Damn B.J. He was getting to her. She needed distance from him. Time to get her head together again.

But hell, that kiss had been something.

When they were younger, she'd never let things get that heated between them. She'd been too afraid that if she gave in, just a little, there would be no stopping point. And wouldn't it be her luck to end up pregnant, no matter how careful she tried to be? No one in town would be surprised. They'd just look at her father and her mother and say, "Figures."

"We're too young," she'd told B.J. whenever his kisses threatened to become a little too intimate. And to his credit, he'd never pushed when she said that.

"I can wait," he'd told her. "But you have to know, I'd never hurt you."

Savannah stared out the kitchen window at the untamed shrubbery. She took another sip of her coffee.

She believed his intentions had been honorable back then. Still, he'd ended up hurting her in an entirely different way.

She sighed. *Be honest here, Savannah. You hurt him, too.*

Savannah closed her eyes. She couldn't see any way to sort out the mess that was her personal life. But she could do her job. She *had* to do her job. How else could she ask the citizens of Bitterroot County to reelect her as their sheriff?

Now that she knew the original investigation had been so shoddy, she couldn't just ignore the fact. It would look as though she was trying to protect her brother. She had to dig further, so she'd be prepared in the case of a reopened investigation.

Last night she'd talked about paying a visit to Sheriff Smith. And while she still felt it was imperative to speak to him, she didn't put it past B.J. to coincidently happen by at just the same moment.

If she wanted to avoid that, then instead of zigging, she needed to zag.

She flipped a few pages in the file, finding the names of the kids who had also driven out to the barn that night. Not that she needed reminding. They'd been her friends back then, too, and she would have been with them that night if her mother hadn't been having an off day. Savannah had decided it wouldn't be safe to leave her eight-year-old sister alone with her.

The gang of friends had traveled in three ATVs to the barn that night, with Hunter and B.J. in the lead. Jonah Clark, Noelle Lewis and Alan Hutchinson had all moved away from the area shortly after high school graduation. Jonah had gone to university in California, where his father had moved after divorcing his mother. Noelle and Alan had got married shortly after they'd both enlisted in the army. Where they were posted now, she hadn't a clue.

That left Hanna White. Hanna still lived in Coffee Creek. She, too, worked at Monahan's Equestrian Center, in the office. She and Savannah had never been close, despite being in the same group of friends.

Hanna had been keen on Hunter, but it was a relationship Savannah hadn't encouraged, as Hanna had been more into parties and boys than school and studying. Still, she'd managed to get a decent job after graduation—and to keep it. In hindsight, Hunter could have done worse than Hanna White.

Savannah gave her old schoolmate a call, not even trying to pretend that it wasn't about business. After a brisk "How are you?" she asked, "I'd like to come by and ask a few questions about the fire eighteen years ago."

She could tell Hanna wanted to say no. But after a few attempts to dissuade Savannah, she finally caved. "If you insist. I usually break for coffee around ten. I can spare you fifteen minutes if you come then."

"I'll be there," Savannah assured her. If her suspicion was right, B.J. would be almost fifty miles away, hoping to ambush her at Sheriff Smith's hobby farm. He'd probably give up around noon, leaving the coast clear for her to move in after her interview with Hanna.

Feeling pleased about her clever planning, Savannah was smiling as she picked up the keys to her SUV and headed for the door.

"Hey there, darlin'." B.J.'s voice lingered over each word as he answered the incoming call on his mobile phone. "She called?"

"Sure did. How did you know?"

"Oh, I have my ways." He'd figured Savannah would be too smart to do the obvious. Still, he couldn't help but smile with satisfaction. It had been eighteen years and he could still read her like a book.

She would hate that.

His smile grew broader.

"What do you want me to tell her when she gets here?"

"Just the truth, darlin'."

"Are you sure? B.J., I'm nervous. I know it's been a long time, but I hate thinking back on that night."

B.J. sobered. "We all do. But don't worry. All you have to do is tell her what you remember. And I'll be right beside you for support."

"I don't think so. Her place is closer than yours. Plus she's had a few minutes' head start."

B.J. took the turn onto the highway. He'd been in Coffee Creek when Hanna White called him, sipping coffee at the Cinnamon Stick. Savannah didn't have the head start. He did.

"Hang tight, Hanna. It's going to be okay."

The Equestrian Center owned by Straws Monahan was a first-class operation specializing in rodeo and riding clinics, including one-on-one training for difficult and troubled horses. The buildings and fencing were a crisp white with red metal roofing on the house and barns. Rows of bright red and white petunias echoed the color scheme on either side of the road leading up to the main entrance. Both the staff and visitor parking lots were quite full, so Savannah left her SUV on the side of the road.

Inside the main building, Savannah asked to speak to Hanna White and was directed to an outdoor area where staff members could relax and have coffee or lunch during their breaks. On her way, she passed Straws himself, returning to his office with a full cup of coffee.

Straws was a tall, slightly paunchy, bow-legged cowboy in his sixties, dressed in black jeans and a starched white shirt with a silver-tipped bolo tie.

"Sheriff." He touched his hat respectfully. "What brings you here today? Official business?"

"I need to question Hanna White about an open file from a while back. She may have seen something that could help me tie up a few loose ends."

He nodded. "By the way, my staff has been telling me good things about your sister. She's a hard worker. Catches on real quick, too. I only wish she could have stayed with us longer."

"Yes." She hesitated, then decided she might as well say what was on her mind.

"Regan *is* smart. We're hoping she gets accepted into medical school this fall. I was disappointed that she asked for such a large chunk of time off work when she should be saving for tuition."

He looked confused. "Time off work, you say?"

"Yes. So she and Murray could go on a holiday."

"Murray St. Clair—yes, he's a good fellow. They seem to have quite the thing for each other, your sister and this young man. But I'm afraid your sister wasn't totally honest when she said she asked for vacation time. She actually resigned. And Murray's on indefinite leave."

"No." She couldn't believe this. Regan had lied?

"We would never give permission for so many days off for a summer position."

Right. She should have realized that herself. "I don't know what to say." Regan had never lied to her before. At least, not that Savannah knew about.

He shrugged. "Kids, huh? I know, I've raised a few of my own. Anyway, you go ahead and talk to Hanna. You know where to find her?"

Savannah nodded, then continued down the

hall toward the courtyard where she'd been directed. Several picnic tables were set up on a nice green lawn, and a handful of people were lounging with drinks and snacks. Savannah stopped abruptly, her thoughts still on the news Straws had told her.

Why hadn't Regan admitted that she'd quit her job? Yes, Savannah would have been upset, but she'd already been upset by the four weeks.

Unless… Could it be there was more to the plan? Maybe Regan and Murray were thinking of eloping?

No. Anything but that. Savannah put out a hand, suddenly dizzy. She needed to calm down. Breathe. She'd phone Regan later. Her sister would have a logical explanation for all this. If only—

"Are you okay?"

Unbelievable. B. J. Lambert stepped up beside her, taking her arm and leading her to a picnic table, where sandy-haired Hanna White was eyeing her nervously over a mug of coffee.

"I—I'm fine." She glanced from B.J. to Hanna, then back again. Deep breath in. Deep breath out. "I guess the heat got to me there."

Hanna and B.J. exchanged skeptical looks. It was only morning and barely sixty-five degrees. Still, B.J. offered to get her some water, and she accepted. She needed a minute to collect her wits.

So much for giving him the slip. Obviously, she'd been outmaneuvered. Damn it. Feeling her breathing return to normal, she took a closer look at Hanna. Now thirty-four, she was still attractive, with her curly sandy-colored hair, lightly freckled skin and clear blue eyes. Though she wore several rings, none of them was a wedding band or an engagement ring.

"How's Hunter?" was the first thing Hanna said.

She couldn't still have a thing for him, could she?

"I wouldn't know." Savannah didn't try to hide her frustration. "I haven't heard from him in six months." She hesitated. "Have you?"

Hanna didn't say anything, just looked away. Maybe she was remembering how Savannah had discouraged her twin brother from dating her when they were younger.

The uncomfortable moment ended when B.J. returned with a glass of refreshingly cold water. Savannah drank it all, surprised to find that she really needed it.

B.J. leaned against the picnic table, crossing one long leg over the other. He looked a tiny bit smug, but mostly concerned. "You sure you're okay?"

She nodded, embarrassed by her moment of weakness and even more by his attention. She wasn't accustomed to people looking out for her. *Don't get used to this feeling. It's probably just an act. And even if it isn't, you know this isn't going anywhere.*

"I'm fine. Thanks for the water. I wasn't expecting to find you here, B.J."

"You should have been," he replied.

He and Hanna exchanged a glance, which Savannah interpreted to mean that they had some sort of secret pact. She sighed. "I guess you two have already gone over your stories, then."

"No." Hanna's light blue eyes didn't seem to be hiding anything. "B.J. said we should wait for you."

Really? She raised her eyebrows in surprise.

"This isn't an attempt at a cover-up," B.J. said. "I'm just doing my part. You asked for my help," he reminded her.

"A request I've tried to rescind several times now."

"Sorry. I'm like one of those genies you

conjure up from an old lamp. Now that I'm here, you're stuck with me."

Do I at least get three wishes? Professionalism wouldn't let Savannah ask the question. Hanna was listening to their exchange with open curiosity. It was time to get this interview back on track.

"Well, Hanna, B.J. may have already told you this, but new evidence has surfaced that may lead to the identification of the man who died in the fire at the Turner barn back when we were high school seniors."

"It has?" Hanna seemed genuinely surprised. "Who was he?"

So they'd been telling the truth when they'd said they hadn't already talked about the case. Savannah was surprised, as well.

And impressed.

"It's just a theory at this stage," she said. "But he may have been Travis McBride, the son of a wealthy man from L.A. Does that name mean anything to you?"

Hanna shook her head in the negative. "What would a guy from L.A. have been doing out on Silver Creek Ranch?"

"Good question." Savannah glanced at B.J., who was listening carefully, and so far, not interfering. "We don't know. But we're trying to find out. Since I wasn't the sheriff back then, it would help if you could tell us—*me*—everything you remember from that night."

"It was a long time ago," she began hesitantly. "Hunter had this idea for a party. Seems he'd been out on a trail ride with B.J. a few weeks earlier and he saw that old barn. He said he had some bottles of vodka stashed away. Enough for a good party. We were supposed to provide the orange juice."

"Why didn't I hear about any of this?" She'd been part of the same gang of friends, after all.

Hanna shrugged. "Hunter didn't want you knowing. Besides, it was organized last minute. Jonah Clark picked me up around ten o'clock on his ATV. Alan Hutchinson and Noelle Lewis were already in another ATV."

"They were dating back then," Savannah recalled.

"Yeah, Alan and Noelle were. But not me and Jonah. I just needed a ride because Hunter was going with B.J. He didn't own his own ATV."

"So there were six of you on three ATVs?" Savannah confirmed.

She nodded. "We had no idea where we were going, so we followed B.J. and Hunter. It was dark when we got to the old barn, very windy and humid. A storm was coming in—

we could hear thunder in the distance. It was spooky." Hanna wrapped her arms around her, as if protecting herself from the unpleasant memory.

"Do you recall the exact time when you arrived at the barn?" Savannah had pulled out her notebook so she could record the key facts.

"No. But the drive was about half an hour, so it must have been around ten-thirty. We all got off our ATVs. B.J. and Hunter were already in the barn, but Noelle and I were hanging back. Neither one of us felt comfortable about being there. Jonah and Alan were trying to convince us to go inside. Alan said something about how it was going to start raining and we'd be better off in the barn."

"Did you hear any of that?" Savannah asked B.J.

"No. Hunter and I were already inside."

Savannah's throat tightened, thinking of her brother and her boyfriend on that fateful night. If only she'd been with them—maybe none of this would have happened. "What were the two of you doing? Did you see or hear the fellow in the loft?"

B.J. hesitated. "No. We were just waiting for the others."

"The guys almost had Noelle and me convinced to go into that eerie old barn," Hanna continued, "when suddenly there was the loudest crack of thunder I've ever heard. I swear it shook the ground we were standing on." Her eyes widened with the memory. "Lightning flashed right afterward. I felt the hair on my arms stand on end and I could see every detail of Alan's face as clearly as if it was daytime. I screamed. I think Noelle must have, too. We ran back to the ATVs and the guys came, too. Even they were freaked out."

"And what about Hunter and B.J.?"

Hanna took a moment to think. Then she shook her head. "I don't remember. I yelled at them to come. I have no idea if they heard me. It started to rain and Jonah hit the gas. I had to hold tight or risk falling off."

"Did you see the barn catch on fire before you left?" According to the official story, that bolt of lightning had started the fire.

"No. But it must have. Right?"

B.J. nodded.

"On the drive home," Savannah continued, "did you ever see the headlights from B.J.'s ATV behind you?"

Hanna paused again. She glanced at B.J., then admitted, "No."

"Do you have any idea what they did after you left?"

"Yes. They drove to Maddie Turner's place to report the fire."

Maddie Turner had confirmed this. Her statement was in the file. But what had happened between the time Jonah, Hanna and the others drove away from the barn and then? It seemed that only B.J. or Hunter could answer that question.

She was back to where she'd started.

Chapter 8

B.J. walked with Savannah out to the parking lot. He could tell she had a lot on her mind, and so did he. When they reached her vehicle, she paused and turned to him.

"Hanna called and told you I was coming, didn't she?"

"Yup."

"And she did this because you asked her to."

"Right again." He couldn't help grinning. "You probably won't appreciate hearing this right now, but you are the damn sexiest sheriff I have ever seen."

"Stop it, B.J. You have to take this seriously."

"Trust me, I am. I wouldn't be here, otherwise." He placed a hand on her door, in the guise of relaxing, but really to prevent her from opening it and driving away.

Savannah probably knew exactly what he was up to, but she didn't order him to move. Instead, she put a boot on the front bumper and leaned her weight into it. "I admit I asked for your help. But you've got to stop shadowing me. People will start to talk. They won't see me as competent if they think I need B. J. Lambert riding shotgun with me."

She was so wrong about that. "Your image isn't that fragile."

He could tell she wasn't convinced. Why didn't she see herself the way he did, the way he was certain others did, too—as a strong person of integrity and honor?

"What was wrong with you when you first arrived? You looked like you were going to faint. And don't give me any nonsense about being too warm."

She grimaced. "I had a word with Straws in the corridor. Last week Regan told me she and her boyfriend, Murray, had taken a four-week leave to go on a road trip. Turns out Regan didn't ask for a leave at all. She quit."

He could see she was really bothered by that. "Why would she lie to you?"

"Probably to prevent me from flying off the handle. Trouble is, I can't help wondering what else she's lying about."

"Why don't you phone her and ask her?"

"I've tried calling her several times. She won't answer. All she does is send me text messages saying they're fine and not to worry."

"That's something."

"Yes. But I still don't get it. Being a doctor is something she's always wanted. Why is she losing her focus now, when she's so close?"

"Maybe she's afraid of failure," he suggested. "Or could be she's fallen in love. I hear that can derail a person."

Savannah glanced at him, then away.

"Do you remember how it feels?" He sure did. In fact, the more time he spent around her, the more he remembered.

"Yes," she said quietly. "But I never let being in love stop me from doing what I thought was right."

"Maybe Regan isn't, either. Could be that her right is a little different than yours, is all."

Savannah let out a long breath. "When did you get so smart?"

"About eighteen years too late, I figure." He eyed her carefully. "Or maybe it isn't too late?"

"I—I don't know what you mean."

"I bet you do." He moved closer to her. "Have you thought about our kiss? Because I sure have. Can't stop thinking about it, actually."

He stepped even closer so he could see her face. Touching her chin, he dipped his head a few inches so they were eye-to-eye.

He could tell she still didn't trust him. But she was weakening. He put a hand on her hip, to see if she would move into him. When she did he almost groaned at how perfect her body felt next to his.

"Tell me," he repeated, touching her chin again. "Have you thought about our kiss?"

"I… Yes. A little."

"And does it bear repeating?" His mouth was an inch from hers as he asked this. For an answer, she closed the final distance, pressing her warm, full lips to his.

Every cell in his body cried out with pleasure. He pulled her in as close as he could and kissed her with no hesitation this time, only full passion. He crushed her rib cage into his, tasted her lips, her tongue, her neck, her soul.

He kissed her as if this would be his last chance.

And, God help him, she kissed him the same way in return.

It wasn't until someone whistled and called out, "Nice work, Sheriff!" that she pulled back.

"Lord, but you mess with my mind, B.J. I'm on duty, damn you."

"It's not your mind I was messing with just then." He brushed a hand over her hair. Wisps were coming out of the long braid that he'd noticed she usually wore to work. "But I am interested in the entire package in the long run."

She examined him cautiously. "What does *long run* mean to you?"

"Same as most people, I figure. My feelings for you were never casual, Savannah. Even when I was seventeen years old, I wanted to marry you."

She groaned, dropping her head to his chest. He cradled her with his arms. "How can you say that?" she asked. "After all these years?"

"Maybe it's because of all the years that have gone by that I can say it. I ask myself why no other woman has made me feel the way you do. The answer seems pretty obvious."

"Oh, B.J. I keep thinking about what Regan said to me the night before she left. How she was tired of too much responsibility and not enough fun."

"That's pretty understandable, coming from a twenty-four-year-old."

"How about a thirty-four-year-old?" She turned her sexy dark eyes up to him.

It was all he could do to resist kissing her again. "I'd say it applies even more at our age."

She nodded. "I do care about you. I guess it's pretty obvious and I'd be a fool to deny it. But the timing couldn't be worse."

"Because of the case?"

"My credibility is on the line."

"But you weren't the sheriff back then."

"I am now. And with new evidence possibly coming to light—how can I ignore that?"

"If you hang tight, a state investigator may be appointed. Then it will be his problem."

"And people will say I turned a blind eye all these years because of my brother." She swallowed, then added, "And you."

She pushed herself out of his arms. "I can't change who my brother is. But I do have the choice of who…to date."

Dating so did not cover the relationship he wanted to have with her. But it seemed she was determined to deny him even that much.

He felt a flash of anger at her damn stubbornness.

"Don't run off."

"I'm not running. This can't work for us. Just drop it, okay?" She reached for the door handle to her vehicle and reluctantly he moved out of her way.

"Are you telling me we have to wait until the investigation is over to be together?"

"I'm not sure we can ever be together. It's just…complicated."

"What if you resigned and we moved somewhere else? We could have a fresh start."

"Are you serious? You'd leave your family? Your ranch?"

"Of course I would. Haven't I been doing just that for the past eighteen years?"

"Well, I'm sorry, but it's not that easy for me. Being sheriff isn't just a job to me. It's who I am."

The sincerity in her voice came through—she truly believed what she was saying.

"Once, I felt the same way," he said, his words measured and calm. "That I was a rodeo cowboy and that was that. But I've learned a job—even one you love—doesn't really define a person. It simply isn't enough."

"And when did that bit of wisdom come to you?"

A few seconds passed before he answered. "When Brock died, I guess."

Just like that, her anger was gone.

"Oh, B.J." She squeezed his upper arm and for a brief second rested her forehead against his shoulder.

"The message took a while to sink in," he added. "And I've spent a bunch of sleepless nights mulling it over. But I finally realized my place is here, helping my family."

"That's good," she said, sounding as though she meant it.

"So you and me…?"

She looked up at him with her intense dark eyes. "I admit I'm tempted. But I'd need to know I can trust you."

"I'd never cheat on you, Savannah. I'm not that kind of man. Maybe you figure my years on the rodeo circuit made me into some kind of ladies' man, but it's not the case."

"I'm not just talking about that." She fixed him with another of her long, measured looks. "You're holding back the truth from me, B.J., and I can't just let that slide." She paused, looking at him expectantly.

B.J. felt hog-tied. If he told her what her brother had done, he'd hurt her and possibly put even more distance between them. "I can't say any more about that night. I need you to trust me that I didn't do anything wrong—nothing more than trespassing, anyway."

She wasn't impressed. "Fine. Be that way. Just don't expect me to be falling into your bed anytime soon. Because it's not going to happen."

Nothing more to be said now. He watched as she got behind the wheel and drove away. He could guess where she would be going next. And much as he figured she wouldn't want him to, he was determined to follow.

Something was happening to her. Savannah stared at the gate in front of her. Somehow she'd driven all the way to Jed and Marissa Smith's ranch without remembering a minute of the drive.

That was because the biggest chunk of her was back with B.J.—reliving their kiss and the words he'd spoken to her afterward.

She'd known he felt something for her, but never guessed he was as serious as that. He had actually mentioned marriage.

B.J. said she should trust him, but how could she when it was obvious he wasn't telling her the whole story? He hadn't then and he wasn't now.

She had to keep reminding herself of this.

And remember that without trust, a relationship had zero chance of being a success.

Savannah turned into the lane that led to the Smiths' pretty log house with the blue metal roof. A goat grazed on the patchy lawn and several chickens were scratching in some dirt at the side of the house. Next to the house was a big vegetable garden, protected from all the animals by a high wire fence.

As soon as she got out of her truck, two midsize dogs came rushing to greet her.

Next the front door opened and a tall, thin woman with dark, sun-aged skin stepped out to the porch. She whistled and the dogs stopped in their tracks, then trotted back to her.

"Savannah! What a nice surprise!" Marissa Smith pulled on gardening gloves, then slipped her feet into the boots that were sitting on a mat by the door.

"I was heading out to hill my potatoes when I heard the dogs making a commotion." She pulled on the collar of one of the dogs—a mongrel breed about the size of a golden retriever. "Calm down, Blaze."

"It's nice to see you, too, Marissa. Your garden looks amazing. I actually dropped by to talk to Jed, if he's available."

"I'm sure he'll be glad to have a chat. He's

in the shop, working on his boat. He's hoping to go fishing this weekend." She pointed to the tall metal building to the right of the house.

"Thanks." Savannah smiled then set out to find Jed. But she hadn't quite reached the shop when a third vehicle pulled into the lane. Marissa had disappeared in the potato patch, but the dogs went out to greet the new visitor.

Savannah wasn't feeling so friendly.

Damn B.J. He was the most stubborn guy she had ever known.

But even more maddening than his refusal to back off was the flutter of happiness she felt at knowing he hadn't.

Jed Smith was sorting through his fishing tackle when Savannah stepped into the shop, B.J. a step behind her. Jed was a large man who'd become at least twenty pounds larger since his retirement. He dropped the lead he'd been holding and turned to Savannah with a welcoming smile.

"Good to see you, Sheriff Moody." Then, noticing the man behind her, he frowned. "And who's that with you? That Bob Lambert's son? The oldest one?"

"Yes, it's me, Sheriff Smith." B.J. walked past Savannah to shake the older man's hand.

It was a shock to see how much he'd aged over the years. Made B.J. wonder what his own father would look like now, if he were still alive.

"I'm not the sheriff anymore, son. You can call me Jed. You sure do look like your old man. He was one of my best friends, you know."

"So…" Jed was eyeing the two of them thoughtfully. "You guys together?"

"No, we are not," Savannah said.

B.J. could see she was pissed off with him. But then, he'd been expecting that.

"He followed me here because the questions I want to ask you have to do with—"

"Let me guess," Jed interrupted, holding up one hand. "The events that took place back when you kids were in high school?"

"That's right, sir." Savannah filled him in with the recent developments. "So it seems our unknown traveler may soon have an identity."

"Frankly, I'm surprised it took so long. Despite the fact that circumstances made him out to be a drunken vagrant, he didn't really look like one. Teeth were too straight and white—hell, even his fingernails were clean. We tried real hard to ID him, though, and had no luck."

"I guess his family thought he'd run off to Mexico. They never thought of looking in Montana."

"I see." Jed Smith put a hand to his chin and rubbed it absentmindedly as he considered the situation. "And you say that watch was pawned *after* the time of death?"

Savannah nodded.

He shook his head sadly. "Damn. I should have known this was going to come back to haunt us."

"I've read over the report you filed back then, sir...."

"And I bet you found it rather incomplete, didn't you?"

"There *are* some unanswered questions."

B.J. didn't envy Savannah her situation. He knew Jed had been her mentor and that she looked up to him. So questioning the thoroughness of his investigation back then had to be difficult for her.

She was being professional and polite, though. And he admired her even more for how well she handled the delicate situation.

"I think this calls for a beer. Anyone else?" Jed crossed the floor to a fridge and pulled out a can. B.J. and Savannah both declined the offer.

Jed popped the tab, took a swallow, then

gestured for them to follow him out a back door to the woodpile. There were four large stumps that provided decent sitting, and Jed waited until they were all settled before saying, "Okay. You have questions. Ask them."

Savannah pulled out a small notebook with worn corners and flipped a few pages. She snapped the end of her pen. "Let's start with this one. According to the report, the fire was started by lightning. Did you have the arson experts out to take a look, though? There's no mention in the files."

Jed rubbed his chin again. "Gotta admit... we didn't call in the team on this one. Given the big storm that night, we just figured it was the most logical thing to assume natural causes for the fire. And of course, the kids had no idea there was anyone in the loft. Or they'd have tried to save him."

Savannah scribbled something in her notebook. B.J. could only imagine what she thought. Even to him, the sheriff's actions back then sounded negligent. He wondered how much the sheriff's friendship with his father had impacted his decisions that night. Had the sheriff not wanted to find answers that might land his friend's son in trouble?

Since his father was dead, and the sheriff

was unlikely to tell him, he supposed he'd never know.

"Okay. Next question," Savannah said briskly. "Assuming our dead guy is Travis McBride, how did he get out to that barn? He obviously didn't drive or you would have found his vehicle. He didn't get a lift with B.J. and Hunter or with the other kids that drove out on their ATVs for the party. Did you question the neighbors to see if anyone had given him a ride or seen him walking along the road?"

"That's a good question, all right. As it happens we did question the neighbors. I didn't put that in the file?"

Savannah shook her head.

"Probably because no one saw anything worth reporting." He shrugged. "I guess the guy could have caught a lift with a trucker, then walked from the highway."

"That's a mighty long walk," Savannah countered.

"Couldn't agree more."

She sighed, jotted something in her notebook, then hit him with her next question. "According to the medical examiner's report, McBride was intoxicated when he died. How did that happen? Did you find any empty bottles with the body?"

"Nope." Jed gave Savannah an approving nod. "These are good, solid questions you're asking. Believe me, I asked them, too, eighteen years ago." He switched his gaze to B.J. "I take it you can't help us out?"

B.J. was glad that he could say with all honesty, "I never saw any bottles. But then, I was never up in the loft."

"Hunter neither, right?" Savannah asked quickly.

He hesitated, even though he knew what he had to say. The lie was no easier now than it had been back then. "Hunter neither."

Savannah's large dark eyes fixed on him, their expression inscrutable. Meanwhile Jed heaved a big sigh.

"So it's all still a big mystery, isn't it?" Jed rubbed the side of his face. "We may know the kid's name and that he had his watch stolen, but why he was at the Turners' barn and how he got there, well, that's something we'll probably never figure out."

For a few moments they were all silent. The squabbling of a robin as it shooed a magpie away from its nest filled the void. They all looked up to watch. Then Savannah finally spoke.

"I guess it's a good thing that fire was started by lightning. Because if the boys

started it, even if they had no knowledge of
the man in the loft, we'd be looking at mitigated homicide."

B.J.'s gut tightened.

"Given the lack of evidence and the pas-
sage of time, I doubt they could put a case
together against these boys," Jed said, not
seeming to realize he was talking about men
who were now in their thirties.

"Maybe not," Savannah agreed. "But we
could hardly blame the McBrides if they
tried, could we?"

As they left the shop at the conclusion
of their conversation with Jed, Savannah
wouldn't even look at B.J.

"I guess we're no further ahead, are we?"
He walked beside her as she made her way
toward her vehicle.

"We?" She whirled on him. "We?"

"Whoa. No need to get all crazy on me."

"I'm not the crazy one. I guess I didn't
make myself clear enough to you earlier. We
are not working on this case together. Period.
Stop following me around. And don't tell me I
dragged you into this. When I asked for your
help, what I meant was that I needed you to
tell me the truth. But that's the one thing you
still haven't done."

Her words hurt. The truth often did. His jaw muscles ached, he was clenching them so hard. He let out a tired breath. "I'm trying to help—the only way I know how."

She looked into his eyes as if she could find in them the answers he wasn't giving her. But she couldn't.

"I wish I could believe you, but there has to be something you're not telling me, because there are some pretty big gaps between the facts of this case and the story that you and Hunter concocted."

She was right—her instincts were on target. But how could he tell her that he'd seen her brother go up that loft? Hunter hadn't been there long—only a minute or two. But it was long enough that he must have seen the man passed out in the corner. Maybe he'd even stolen the watch.

One thing was for sure. Hunter had seemed agitated when he climbed down from the ladder, and the crazy, loud boom of thunder had spooked him further.

"Let's get out of here!" he'd cried. He'd pulled on B.J.'s arm and dragged him outside, just as the rain had started to fall. A second later the lightning hit, igniting the barn and making their skin tingle.

He and Hunter had raced for the ATV,

nearly choking from panic. B.J. had just one thought on his mind. He had to phone the fire department. He'd headed to the nearest house—which happened to be Maddie Turner's.

This was the truth. It was something he'd tried to block from his mind for eighteen years. And now Savannah wanted him to unload his nightmare onto her.

He didn't want to do it. He knew how much it would hurt her. She probably wouldn't even believe him. For sure Hunter wouldn't back him up. He'd claim B.J. was lying. That *he'd* been the one who'd been up in the loft.

No matter how he thought this through, B.J. couldn't see a way out.

"I've told you everything that I can." Seeing she was about to get into her vehicle, he realized he had to give her more. A small kernel of the truth that she could hang on to. "I didn't know that guy, Savannah. And I have no idea how he got to the barn. If I'd realized he was up there, I would have tried to save him when that fire started. I would have."

She stared at him for a long moment. "I wish I could believe you."

Then she got behind the wheel and drove

off. He swore, kicked his front tire, then followed behind her all the way back to Coffee Creek.

When they reached the town, Savannah headed for her office. B.J. turned onto Main and angle-parked in front of the Cinnamon Stick. A sandwich and some black coffee would give him the fortification he needed for the next job he intended to do.

It had been a hellish day so far. Why not complete the fun with a visit to his long-estranged aunt?

Laurel was at the counter this afternoon, her long red hair up in a messy bun as she cleared dishes from the counter. She gave him a warm smile when she saw him, and he had no trouble seeing why his brother had fallen for her at first sight.

"Hey, Laurel. Where's the munchkin?"

She gestured to a playpen in the corner. "Napping. I usually take her upstairs, but she dropped off before I had a chance."

He settled on the first of three vacant stools, feeling the tension slip out of his shoulders. This place had a good, homey vibe. "Hope your day is going better than mine."

His sister-in-law tucked a strand of hair behind her ear and gave him a shake of her head. "Judging by the looks of you, I'd say it definitely is. Would you like your coffee in a cup or should I set up an IV line?"

He chuckled. A good sense of humor was one of the things he most liked about Corb's new bride. "Maybe both. Plus a sandwich." He glanced at the chalkboard to his right. "The daily special would be fine."

"Ham, cheese and tomato coming right up." She passed him a large-size, take-out cup of steaming, fresh coffee. "Heading home now?"

"Eventually. First I'm planning to pay a visit to Maddie Turner."

"Really? Corb wants to do that, too. We're hoping to find some time to go together next week. I think he's a little nervous about it. The family feud has always bothered him a lot."

"Me, too. I'll sleep better once I've done what I can to mend fences. But for all I know, she'll boot me off the property before I get a chance to apologize."

"Surely not."

"Even if she doesn't, I'm still not sure what to say to her. How can I explain why I've behaved like such an asshole all these years?"

"You can start by saying exactly that." Vince came out of the kitchen at that moment, stripping off his apron and dropping it into a basket near the back door. "My shift is over, but if you're planning to visit Maddie, would you take her some cinnamon buns? She loves them and she hasn't been well enough to come to the café in a long while."

As he spoke Vince was boxing a half dozen of the sticky rolls. When he was done, he taped the box closed and handed it to B.J.

"Sure I will, but—" B.J. did some math and realized Vince and Maddie must be close to the same age. "I didn't realize you knew my aunt."

"Well, I did. And if I'd have been a smarter man, I would have married her. But I picked the rodeo instead. And the bottle." He turned to Laurel. "See you tomorrow."

And then he was gone out the back door and B.J. was left staring at Laurel, who looked as amazed as he felt.

"Vince Butterfield and Maddie Turner," she said slowly. "Who would have guessed?"

"Not me," he assured her. His visit with his aunt was going to be even more interesting than he'd thought.

Chapter 9

The last time B.J. had been to his aunt's house—the only time—was eighteen years ago. He'd knocked urgently on her door, and as soon as she'd opened it, had yelled at her to call 911. "Your old barn is on fire!"

He remembered how wide her eyes had gone. "You okay?" she'd asked. Two dogs tried to push their way outside and she'd closed the door to a small gap as she waited for his answer.

"Yeah."

"Good. Go home now, B.J. And tell your father." Then she'd shut the door firmly.

Now B.J. stood in front of that same door. It needed staining. The bottom panel had started to rot. He thought of the countless bulls and broncos he'd faced in his rodeo career. How odd that he'd never felt nearly as nervous in the chute as he did right now.

It was five o'clock. She might be out in the barns doing chores. Or starting her supper. He hadn't thought of it before, but this wasn't the most convenient time to pay a visit. Maybe he should come back tomorrow....

And then he heard something come up from his rear. A border collie—younger than Sky and a little smaller—was sniffing his leg. Then a second dog, very similar to the first, had her nose on B.J.'s boot.

"Honey. Trix."

Both dogs lifted their heads, then promptly ran toward their mistress. B.J. swung around slowly.

His aunt was walking from the barn toward him. Maddie had on baggy overalls, with a long-sleeved shirt and a checkered bandanna tied at her throat. She didn't look much like his mother. Except, he realized as she drew closer, for her eyes.

They were the trademark Turner green— the color of a glacier-fed lake in the summer time.

Her complexion was gray, and the skin at

her cheeks and jaw was slack, suggesting a recent loss of weight.

She stopped when they were about ten feet apart. The dogs halted, too, one on either side of her, heads swiveling from their mistress to the stranger, then back to Maddie.

She calmed them with a hand to each of their heads. Tipping her own head to one side, she regarded him for several seconds before lifting her chin. "You here to talk me out of giving my land to Jackson?"

"God, no." His reply was instinctive and swift.

"Good. You can come inside, then. Want some supper?"

She led him into a spacious kitchen that belonged to another era—well before granite and stainless steel. The flooring and counters were of aged pine, and the stove was an antique wood-burning model that even on this warm summer evening was putting out a modicum of heat.

"Don't use electric," Maddie explained as she added a log to the stove, then put a kettle on to boil. Two cats were suddenly in the room. Whether they'd been sleeping in some quiet corner or had sneaked through one of the two doors, B.J. couldn't say. One of them slunk up against his leg. The other hung back and watched the proceedings with sleepy eyes.

It was a cozy room. Chaotic but welcoming. There were braided rugs on the floor and hand-sewn cushions on the chairs.

Before he knew it Maddie had fried up potatoes, sausages and onions and had a plate of food on either end of the painted wood table.

"I'm sorry about your brother Brock," Maddie said.

He accepted her commiserations with a nod. "And I was sorry to hear you were sick. Sure made me think, though. Just seems crazy that we spent our entire lives living a few miles apart and yet stayed so—"

"Separate." Maddie supplied a word that seemed to fit.

She had a fork in hand but had yet to put any food in her mouth, even though it smelled delicious. B.J. took a taste and confirmed that this was so.

"You kids were caught in the middle of an ugly situation. As your aunt, I had to watch you grow up from afar. Don't think I blame you for that. I'm leaving my land to Jackson for another reason entirely."

"We're going to miss him at Coffee Creek. But at least he isn't going far."

"Don't think I poached him from you without any scruples. But you have to agree—I need him more than your family does right now. Besides—that young man needs some space from the Lamberts. He's suffered a lot since that accident."

"He blames himself, doesn't he? But the facts are clear—he wasn't at fault."

"Logic has little to do with our emotions, young man. I learned that lesson long ago."

B.J.'s plate was empty, yet she'd barely touched her dinner. Still, she stood as if the meal was over. "Want to see some pictures?"

He did. He followed her to the next room, which was dominated by a dark mahogany table and half a dozen chairs—all covered with plastic. On the wall were many photographs in ornate silver frames.

She pointed out a couple in wedding apparel. "My parents. Your grandmother and grandfather."

He could hardly make out their features. But a later photo of the couple with a two-year-old daughter in the father's arms was clearer. His grandmother Turner was a ringer for his own mother at that age. She was obviously pregnant, posing with her hands resting on the large mound of her baby.

"That's the last picture we have of her." Maddie sounded sad, even though she was talking about events that had happened over sixty years ago. "She went into labor about a month after this was taken, and, well, I'm sure you know what happened."

He did. His grandmother had given birth to a healthy baby girl—his mother—but she herself had not survived.

"She looks so much like my mother."

"Yes. Olive was lucky. I took after my father." Maddie shrugged, obviously not too bothered by the fates that had made one daughter slender and pretty, the other stocky and plain.

B.J. hesitated, a question hovering in his mind. Should he just ask? Maddie seemed pretty open.

"You want to know what went wrong?" Maddie asked shrewdly. "Why two sisters got so riled up that they spent the past forty years not talking to one another?"

"Corb says it had something to do with Grandpa Turner. That our mother didn't have a chance to say her goodbyes before he died. And that she blames you for that."

"Really? Is that what Olive told you?" Maddie looked disgusted, then sad. "Well, I suppose it doesn't matter. Not anymore."

B.J. couldn't accept that. "It does matter. To me, anyway."

Maddie shook her head. "I always promised myself that if any of you kids ever made any overtures to me, I wouldn't try to drive a wedge between you and your mother. And what would be the point now, anyway?"

He supposed she was referring to her disease and the limited amount of time she had left. "Shouldn't the truth always matter?"

As soon as he'd spoken the words, he realized what a hypocrite he was being. Lucky thing Savannah hadn't heard him.

"Truth is important. But it's not the only factor to consider." She moved on to the next family picture, taken when both sisters were older, around six and eight.

"This is my mother?"

"Yes."

Grandpa Turner had his arm around Maddie's shoulders, while Olive stood slightly apart, shoulders hunched, expression aggrieved. There were other photos. Some of the girls together. Others with their father.

Whenever the family was shot as a whole, he noticed Grandpa Turner had a hand on Maddie, but never his mother.

His mother had always claimed that *she* was her father's favorite. But an ugly idea occurred to him. "Did Grandpa Turner blame my mother for Grandma's death?"

Maddie's face grew sadder. "It wasn't logical. But that's what I was trying to explain to you earlier, Robert. Emotions and logic all too often have nothing to do with one another."

She let out a sigh. "It's been nice chatting with you. But I need to lie down now."

He took the hint. But when he got to his truck, he saw the box from the Cinnamon Stick. Shoot, he'd forgotten to give Maddie her buns. He grabbed the box then hurried back to the house, rapping lightly on the door before letting himself inside.

Maddie was sitting, arms on the table, head resting on the pillow they made.

"Are you all right?"

She lifted her head. "Just tired." Her gaze went to the white box in his hands. "What's that?"

"Vince Butterfield asked me to bring these to you."

Damn if a flush didn't rise on his aunt's cheeks. B.J. set the cinnamon buns on the table near enough that she could reach them without stretching.

"Even after all these years, I guess he's still sweet on you."

Maddie looked at him sharply. "What would you know about that?"

"Just what he told me. That he chose the

rodeo rather than marrying you. And that it was the biggest mistake of his life."

"He said that?" she whispered. "I always thought…"

"What?"

"Never mind. Thanks for bringing these, B.J. And if you ever feel like another visit, I'd be glad to see you."

B.J. didn't make it back to the ranch until almost seven that evening. He had a lot on his mind and didn't notice his brother until Corb slapped a hand on his back.

"Showing up a little late for evening chores." Corb looked tired, and B.J. felt suddenly guilty.

"Sorry about that. I got tied up with Savannah today. Then I stopped in to see Maddie."

"That's real nice, B.J., but the horses still need to be fed and watered around here."

"I'll get right on it—"

"Don't bother. Jay—" one of the hired hands "—and I just finished doing your work for you."

"Thanks. I owe you."

"I don't mind. But Laurel might. After a long day at the café and looking after Stephanie, she really counts on me getting home by six."

"Is there something on your list that I can take care of so you can have a few extra hours in the morning with your family?"

Corb's expression softened. "Not to worry. Just carry your weight from here on in. Mom's real excited about you coming home. So am I. We're hoping it works out for all of us."

B.J. stood his ground watching as his brother drove the ATV toward his home. Corb's words had him thinking. Was he on probation here?

Hell. Seemed as though Savannah wasn't the only one who didn't trust him.

Savannah spent most of the next day in her office. She had some admin matters to take care of. She also tracked down Jonah, Noelle and Alan by phone and asked them what they remembered about that night. Not one of them had anything helpful to add to the information Hanna had already given her.

The day went by slower than usual. Savannah started whenever the phone rang or someone knocked on her office door. She didn't want to admit it, but the reason was clear.

She kept expecting B.J. to show up.

So far, she'd seen him every day since he'd moved back to Coffee Creek.

So why not today?

Was he regretting that kiss in the Monahan's parking lot? She sure was.

And yet, she felt a thrill every time she thought about it.

And she thought about it far, far, too often.

Eventually, at five o'clock, she decided she'd had enough. She had more work to do, but she needed a change of scene. Packing some budget papers into her leather bag, she locked up and headed out to her SUV.

She hadn't driven beyond the town limits when her phone went off.

The quick lift of her spirits flattened when she saw that the call was from her mother. Deciding it was a sign that she'd better make a visit, she told her mother to hang up—she'd be there in five minutes and they could talk in person.

But when she arrived at the rest home she found that her mother was not in one of her more lucid moods. Francine started babbling as soon as Savannah stepped into her room. She was in her chair, looking out the window at the topaz-colored water of Coffee Creek.

"I was just thinking about the farm," she said. "That damn flood has ruined all the crops, and now the bank is threatening to foreclose on us. What are we going to do?"

She was lost in movie land again, pretending she was Sissy Spacek in the 1984 movie *The River*.

"It'll be okay, Mom. The bank won't foreclose."

"I hope you're right." Francine pressed a hand to her forehead. "I'm so tired. Help me to my bed, won't you, dear?"

Ten minutes later Savannah was back on the road, depressed after her aborted visit with her mother. She'd left Francine sleeping peacefully with a smile on her face, finally convinced that they weren't going to lose the farm, after all.

Her mother's ability to differentiate between reality and fantasy was blurring more and more with time. It wasn't an easy thing for a daughter to witness, especially since her mother's doctor assured her that there was no physical cause for her mother's form of mental illness. And at age fifty-eight it was much too early for senility to be setting in.

Savannah headed back to her acreage, not looking forward to spending the evening alone. Now that Regan was gone, home had become a place to avoid.

As soon as she turned in her lane she saw that something was different.

The rusted-out trucks were gone.

She drove farther, and then saw B.J.'s

truck. He had the tailgate down and was sitting there, obviously waiting for her.

It scared her how happy she felt to see him.

She parked her SUV and waited a few seconds before switching off the ignition. How should she handle this? She had to be cool.

But then he gave her a smile and she couldn't help responding in kind.

"I took the liberty of bringing over dinner." He removed a wicker picnic basket from the truck and started toward her house. "You okay with eating on the porch?"

She stared at the basket. "Dinner?"

"I couldn't risk you offering me one of those frozen entrées again, could I?" He sat in a cushioned chair and started pulling items out of the basket. A couple of beers, beaded with moisture. A roasted chicken, already carved. Biscuits. Potato salad.

A million calories, Savannah thought.

A million delicious calories.

She could get all affronted and tell him she had plans, that he had no right to be on her property, uninvited. Instead, she took the chair to his right and accepted the beer that he had just opened.

"Any new word on the case?"

"No."

"Maybe that's a good thing."

"Maybe." She sipped her beer, then relaxed her back into the chair. Beside her, B.J. did the same, stretching out his long legs to the point that his boot touched the side of hers.

She didn't move away from the contact.

He was so damn handsome. She'd forgotten what it was like to be so close to him. At one time he'd been such a constant presence in her life that she'd almost taken him for granted. But that had been a long time ago.

Things were different with them now. There was no going back.

"I talked to Noelle, Jonah and Alan. None of them remembered anything more than Hanna. Not that I expected them to." After this many years that probably meant that they were telling the truth. Whatever had happened in the barn that night, only B.J. and Hunter knew for sure.

She narrowed her eyes as she watched him fill a plastic plate with food. Unless there'd been a third person there that night. Someone who didn't know the kids were planning a party…

But no. The kids would have seen his vehicle. Savannah sighed. She was back where she'd started, with no rational explanation for what had happened.

"You look like you're thinking too hard."

B.J. passed her the plate of food, then filled a second one with a serving for himself.

The food smelled great and tasted better. Between mouthfuls she asked, "So what happened to the trucks?"

"Corb and I hauled them to the salvage yard in Lewistown this afternoon."

"All the way to Lewistown?" It must have taken them a couple of hours. She'd tried before to have the vehicles towed, but because they didn't have engines she would have had to pay big bucks. "Why?"

"You told me they were eyesores, right?"

"Yes."

"And Lewistown has the closest salvage yard."

"But that was my mess to clean up." Bad enough that he'd done this for her, but he'd also enlisted his brother.

"It just seemed to me that you could use a hand. That's all."

Savannah prided herself on her independence. Asking for help wasn't something she ever did. And accepting it when it was freely offered was almost as difficult.

"You didn't have to do that."

"You're making that pretty clear."

"This better not have anything to do with that kiss at Monahan's the other day. I am not open to a relationship right now. And even if I were, it definitely wouldn't be with you."

B.J. set aside his food and met her gaze calmly. "Is that so?"

"It is."

"So, you're not attracted to me. Is that what you're saying?"

The brute. He knew she'd kissed him back with a passion that had equaled his own. "That's not the point."

"Oh?"

"A good relationship is grounded in respect and trust. We don't have that."

"You don't respect me?"

"Damn it, B.J. Why are you making this so hard?"

She got up from the chair, paced to the end of the porch then swung around.

"I'm not giving up on us, Savannah. I recognize you've got reasons to question what I told you about that night. But I don't see why that should matter. I didn't do anything wrong. Why won't you believe me?"

"Because if you didn't do anything wrong, then that means Hunter did."

B.J. froze. He hadn't meant her to draw that conclusion. But he could see why she had. Especially since it was the truth.

"Have you thought of talking to your brother about this?"

"I've been sending him emails every day since I got home from Oregon. He still hasn't gotten in touch and I'm not ready to stoop to official channels." She sighed.

"Want me to try and find him?"

B.J. was standing now, too, looking at her with an expression that seemed full of compassion.

Damn him. She didn't need his sympathy. She blinked away tears. God help her, she didn't want to start crying. Why hadn't she run him off her land right from the start? "Would you stop being so damn nice?"

He shook his head. Any other woman and he'd be long gone. "I just can't win with you, can I?"

Chapter 10

Somehow, despite his best intentions, the evening had gone sideways. B.J. hated seeing Savannah so upset. He'd only wanted to make her happy by getting rid of those old junk heaps and bringing her a decent dinner.

Instead, she was all worked up.

And determined to see him as the bad guy.

Even if she knew the truth about the night of the fire, he doubted it would make any difference. She still blamed him for the party, for the fire, for *everything*. Her protective instincts and loyalty would always belong to her brother first.

He couldn't blame her for that. She'd been looking out for Regan and Hunter most of her life. But there was never anyone to look out for *her*.

How could he make her understand that he wanted to be the one to do that? Every instinct he possessed was telling him to take her into his arms. But she was still looking at him as if he was the enemy.

"You shouldn't have let it happen in the first place."

There were back to this.

"That night was a huge mistake. But we were kids. A lot has changed since then, but my feelings for you haven't."

He moved even closer, searching her eyes to see if his words were reaching her at all. When he saw the glistening of fresh tears, he put his arms around her.

She pushed back for a second.

And then she wrapped her arms around his neck and clung to him with a desperation that matched his own.

"B.J....?"

He kissed her, because that seemed the only answer that would tell her what she needed to know about him. That he was here, and he was hers, and she could count on him.

She was on her toes now, sliding her hands from his shoulders to his back. Her kisses told him that she still cared, too. And that she was willing to give him a second chance.

They hadn't been lovers the first time. They'd been too young.

But they were adults now and his need for her was desperate. He pressed her body snug against his, and she drove him crazy when she gave a sexy wiggle of her hips.

He brushed her hair back so he could see her face. "Sweetheart?"

She knew what he was asking. "Let's take this inside…."

He shouldered open the door, not quite believing this was really happening. Savannah was in his arms, kissing him as madly as he was kissing her.

And then she had his hand and was leading him down a narrow hall. He glimpsed a room with white walls and a neatly made bed. In his mind he was already lowering Savannah onto the pale blue quilt when her cell phone rang.

She unclipped it from her belt and placed it on a wooden bureau near the door. Her shirt had come untucked and he took the opportunity to rest his hands on her bare waist. Her skin was smooth and he followed the curves of her hips down to the leather belt that was part of her uniform.

This would have to go.

He was working the buckle when the landline rang. Savannah tensed, and he gave a mental curse, already understanding that she'd decided to take the call.

"Hang on." She placed a kiss on his lips, then pushed against his chest until he dropped his arms. There was a handset on the bedside table and she reached for it with one hand, while the other smoothed down her wild hair.

"Yes?" Her eyes were bright and locked with his. He went to her, sliding his hands around her waist again, but she shook him off and turned her back.

"When?" She was tucking in her shirt now as she continued to listen.

He felt as if he'd been slammed into a brick wall. Retreating from the room, he found himself in the kitchen. A postcard with a picture of Chicago's skyline was on the table next to a stack of junk mail. Without thinking, he flipped it over.

Having a great time. Don't worry. Love you, Regan.

The murmur of Savannah's voice carried down the short hall. "Thanks, Paul. I appreciate the call." Then a few seconds later, he heard her say, "Maybe. I'll let you know."

She was in the kitchen a few seconds after

that. The color was still high in her lips and on her cheeks, but her clothing was back in place and her eyes broadcast the need for extreme caution.

"Who was that?"

Her gaze dropped from him to the table. "Paul Corrigan. He's a deputy attorney from the county attorney's office."

There was something about the way she'd said the man's name that made him wonder. The chill in his heart suddenly became colder. "And?"

Finally she met his gaze. "They have the court order. The body is going to be exhumed tomorrow."

There had never been a woman who could mess with his mind the way Savannah Moody could. And B.J. resented this fact. He had work to do, damn it.

It was early, before dawn, and he was already on his way to the quarter-horse barns. June was still breeding season, and while the hired hands knew what they were doing, it was high time he started contributing more than just the occasional hour or two of work.

He stopped by the stallion quarters to say good morning to Big Shot. The red dun stallion was the king around here, and he sure knew it. He nickered loudly as B.J. approached his stall, tossing his mane and raising his head as if to say, *Finally!*

B.J. measured out his oats and fed the impatient stallion, then moved on to the others. When he was done, he headed for the office to review the breeding charts and schedules.

It was one thing to offer to take over the job of managing the quarter-horse operation—quite another to actually do it. Back when he was a kid living at home, they'd concentrated on cattle—so he wasn't as knowledgeable about his mother's new venture as he'd let on to Jackson.

But he was a quick study.

In the office he put on a pot of coffee and spent the next hour going through files. When hired hands Jay Owen and Griff Benson showed up, he told them that he wanted to hear their thoughts about the operation. Were there any places improvement was needed?

Both nodded thoughtfully and promised to get back to him after they'd finished their morning chores.

By ten o'clock, B.J. had put in five hours' work. And still hadn't eaten breakfast.

Corb came by just at the right time. "Want to join me and Mom up at the house? Bonny usually makes pancakes on Friday."

His mouth started watering on the spot. "You bet." He stuck the lineage papers back into the binder, then joined his younger brother on the walk up to the main house.

His brother was an inch shorter, but strong and sure-footed. His thick blond hair had grown back since the accident but the tip of a scar was still visible.

"You still getting headaches?" Thank God Corb had come out of that coma. B.J. didn't know if he could have survived losing both of his brothers.

"Nope. All healed up, except for this beauty mark." Corb touched a finger to the scar. "Laurel assures me it's sexy."

B.J. laughed. "Yeah, right. What about your memory? Did any of that ever come back?"

Corb shook his head. "The week before the accident is still pretty much a blank slate. The doctor figures if I haven't recalled anything by now I probably never will. It was a problem at first, since I couldn't remember meeting Laurel. But now that we're married, it doesn't matter so much."

They were at the house now, and the delicious aroma of hotcakes and maple syrup had both of them picking up their pace. They washed at the sink, then went to join their mother at the dining table.

Bonny must have been waiting for them, because a moment later she was bringing in the hotcakes, a dish of sausages and a carafe of strong coffee.

As soon as he saw his mother—hair styled and face all made up despite the fact that she was dressed to work—B.J. thought about Maddie. The differences between the two sisters were remarkable.

He wolfed through two plates of breakfast before he decided to raise a delicate topic.

"Mom, are you aware that your sister has lung cancer?"

Her fork clattered to the plate. "What are you talking about, B.J.?"

"Your sister, Maddie. You left the other day without listening to Jackson's explanation for why he's going to work for her. Among other things, he plans to live with her in her house so she doesn't have to go to a hospice to die."

His words were blunt to the point of cruelty, but Olive showed no sign of being affected by her sister's imminent death.

"I'm sorry for Maddie. But she's made her bed." Olive pressed her lips together. "Don't tell me you're planning to go and work for her, too?"

"Of course not. But I did want the chance to meet her before it was too late." He waited for his mother to make the obvious extrapolation. If she and Maddie were ever to reconcile, now was the time.

But Olive showed no sign that her thoughts were moving in that direction. Smoothly she changed the conversation to another topic. "By the way, I'm trying to get Cassidy and Farley to set a date for their wedding. Now that she's moved in with him, it's only right they make it official."

"She's wearing Farley's ring," Corb pointed out. "I'm sure they'll set a date when they're ready."

Olive just shook her head. "Maybe I'd better go out to lunch with that girl next week. A little prodding is what she needs."

With that, Olive set down her napkin, then left the room.

"You warning Cass, or should I?" Corb asked.

B.J. grinned. "I'm thinking we'd best stay out of it."

Standing up on a hill, well back from the action, Savannah glanced from her watch to the sky. At eleven in the morning the day was ridiculously sunny and warm. Not at all the right mood for an exhumation. The solemnity of the occasion called for rain. Or at least a few dark, heavy clouds.

But, no, the Montana sky was as blue as the walls of a little boy's nursery today. A color of hope and optimism. Not death and disappointment.

But why had she thought of that metaphor? Children were not in Savannah's life plan. She felt as if she'd been a mother forever... to her brother and younger sister. And only when Regan was safely in medical school would she feel that her job as surrogate parent was finally done.

"Okay. Good. Bring it up now." Two men, one operating the machinery, the other giving instructions, were doing the work of raising the coffin out of the earth. Watching was an environmental-safety official from Lewistown, as well as June Savage—representing the McBride family—and Paul Corrigan.

Paul and June had been talking during most of the proceedings. Now, as the workers transferred the coffin into a waiting ambulance for transportation to the medical examiner's office in Lewistown, Paul started heading up the hill toward her.

Savannah leaned her weight back on her heels. She wasn't happy that Paul had been assigned this case. This was her turf, after all. But at least she and Paul had history, and having an in on the investigation might prove helpful.

Paul was halfway up the hill when she sensed someone else approaching from her rear. She'd been expecting him and didn't bother turning to verify his identity before speaking.

"Who told you where I was this time?"

"It was Laurel," B.J. said, just before stepping in line beside her. He looked tired, but that only made her want to reach out to him all the more. She clamped down on the impulse.

"The guys hired for the exhumation stopped at the Cinnamon Stick first for coffee," he elaborated.

Savannah shook her head. Good luck keeping a secret in this town.

"So who's that guy?" B.J. nodded toward Paul. He was almost up the hill now and the deputy attorney's face was perspiring lightly, although the fabric of his suit was as pristine as if it had just come off the hanger.

"That's Paul Corrigan."

"Figures," B.J. snorted.

Finally Paul approached them. He looked from her to B.J., then back at her. "Good to see you, Savannah."

"You, too." After a second's pause, she held out her hand. He seemed surprised by the move, but went through the formal ritual of shaking before turning to B.J. "And you are?"

"B. J. Lambert." His voice came out even deeper than usual.

Paul's eyebrows rose. "Really? So you were there the night our John Doe died."

"I was."

"If this ID pans out, you better get yourself a good lawyer. The family is looking for blood."

B.J. made use of the extra couple of inches he had over Paul and managed to look down at him. "Is there such a thing as a good lawyer?"

Paul gave a short, unamused snort. "Right. Good one, Mr. Lambert." He brushed his hands against the fabric on his legs, then turned back to Savannah. "We have the dental records in hand. It won't take more than a day or two to determine whether this really is Travis McBride."

"You'll let me know?"

"As soon as I find out, I'll call," he promised, squeezing her arm lightly. B.J. stepped up between them, jostling Paul's arm and generally making his larger size very evident.

Savannah wanted to smack him. Testosterone could be so annoying. Instead, she opted to ignore him. "I've got to get back to my office. I'll talk to you soon, Paul."

Stepping past B.J. as if he were a cement marker in her path, she headed toward her SUV, leaving Paul to wait for June, who was on her way up the hill now, too.

Of course, B.J. wouldn't let it rest and go about his own business. He followed her until they were out of Paul's hearing and then he started ranting. "What's up with that guy? He was acting like he had some sort of prior claim on you or something."

"Are you asking if Paul and I ever dated? If so, then yes, we did go out for a while. Now maybe *you* can answer a question for *me*." She whirled on him, fighting back another urge to punch his broad shoulder. "What right did you have to act the part of the jealous lover? God, you did everything but pop him one in the face."

"I thought about it," B.J. admitted.

"Seriously?"

"Yeah, seriously. If he hadn't interrupted us last night, we *would* be lovers by now and you know it."

"Well, it's a darn good thing he called then. I'd say his timing was absolutely perfect."

B.J. shot her a look of affronted disbelief.

"Damn it, woman. You drive me crazy. I'm thinking we're finally getting somewhere and here you are jamming on the brakes again."

He was right. She hadn't been behaving rationally around him. And it wasn't like her. She was known for keeping a cool head in a crisis. It was an essential part of her personality.

What was happening to her? Was she losing her sanity…like her mother?

"Hey. Don't look like that." B.J. was suddenly contrite, lowering his head to check her expression. "I didn't mean to yell at you. Are you okay?"

Hell, there were *tears* in her eyes again. She shook her head, not sure how to answer him. When he held out his arms, she shook her head again. She *wanted* to feel his arms around her.

But— "I'm afraid," she admitted.

She'd been alone for so long. She wasn't sure she knew any other way to be. Dating Paul, and the other men who had come in and out of her life in the past eighteen years, had never threatened her peace of mind the way the idea of being with B.J. did.

What they felt for each other…it was just too strong.

"I'm afraid, too."

She was shocked that he would admit it out loud like that. B.J. acted as if nothing on this earth could frighten him.

And yet, apparently, a relationship with her did.

"The crazy thing is, we both take chances almost every day. You're a sheriff. I ride crazy broncos and bulls for a living. We're not cowards."

"That's true," she said, even though she wasn't sure. Being brave on the job was one thing. Risking your heart, another.

"So let's give this thing between us a chance. We can take it slow. Let me take you out to dinner?"

She wanted to say yes. She wanted to reach out to him, the way he was reaching out to her.

But was it the smart thing to do? Was it the *respectable* thing? She had so much on the line. Her job. Her reputation.

Her heart.

"I've got to think about this, B.J. Give me a few days."

"Hell, Savannah." He shook his head, clearly disappointed.

But he didn't argue with her anymore. Just got in his truck and left.

Chapter 11

She was giving him the runaround something awful. Any other woman and he'd think she was playing games.

But Savannah wasn't like that.

B.J. threw himself into his work—the best cure for heartache that he knew. Fortunately, there was plenty of that to be done. The next day he spent almost four hours with Dan Farley, helping the vet preg test the Coffee Creek Ranch mares. B.J. needed to know for sure which ones were pregnant and which ones still had to be bred.

When the job was done and they were leaving the mare barn, he asked the vet if he wanted a beer. "I could grab a couple from the house if you have a few minutes."

"Is your mother home?" was Farley's peculiar response.

"I think so. Why?"

"I'd rather not run into her if I can help it. She'll only be after me about setting the wedding date."

B.J. grinned. "What's the problem? Getting cold feet about marrying my sister?" Fat chance of that happening. He knew damn well that Farley had been in love with Cassidy for half of his life.

"Cass can't make up her mind. One minute she wants to elope. The next, she wants a big do. The rest of the time she talks about a small family affair."

"And what do you want?"

"To marry Cassidy" was his simple, but heartfelt answer.

B.J. walked Farley to his vet truck then saw his old friend safely off before heading to the house to wash up. It was a good thing Farley had left when he did, because Olive was working on her laptop at the kitchen counter, trolling websites, looking for a new stallion, he supposed.

The two of them had talked about this last night. B.J. had showed her his analysis and explained his rationale for thinking it was time for them to invest in another stallion. It seemed his mother had been convinced if she was already shopping.

"Find any good prospects?" He grabbed a beer from the fridge and a leftover sandwich from the tray Bonny had made for lunch.

"Well, there's Amber Ellis. She dated Farley a bit, but they were never serious."

"Huh?" He plopped down on the stool next to his mom's and took a look at the computer screen. Hell! His mother was on a dating site. "I thought you were searching for our new stallion."

"Word's going around that you were kissing Sheriff Moody in Monahan's parking lot last week." His mother looked at him reproachfully.

"Are you kidding me? Mom, I mean this in the nicest way possible, but it's none of your business who I kiss."

"But have you considered her background? Her father was a gambler and a drinker. And her mother is mentally ill. For all we know the problem is genetic."

B.J. stared at his mother, dumbfounded that she would judge an amazing woman like Savannah based on the weaknesses of her parents. For the first time he realized that

Savannah's concerns about her reputation weren't entirely groundless.

How many other people thought the way his mother did?

"She's a good person, Mom."

"I'm not saying she isn't. Just that you can do better."

Suddenly he made the connection. "Are you on that site looking for someone for *me?*"

"Don't look so insulted. *Everyone* uses internet dating sites these days. And Amber—"

"Mom." He held up his hand. "Hold it right there. Corb may put up with your meddling ways, but I won't."

His mother flinched at the word *meddling.* "I just want you to be happy, son."

B.J. steeled himself against the waver in her voice. He knew his mother's tricks. And he wasn't giving in to them. He loved his mom and she'd been a good parent in many ways. When he was young, she'd always been there, nursing him when he was sick, helping with the school projects he'd always left to the last minute.

But life had been easier when their father was alive. Calm, steady Bob Lambert had known how to keep his more emotional wife on an even keel. Without his influence, Olive could easily get carried away.

"I appreciate your concern, Mom. But I'm thirty-four years old. How would you like it if I told *you* who to date?"

"Me? Date?"

"Why not? Dad's been gone a long time. And you're still an attractive woman."

He could tell that his last comment pleased her.

"Well. I must admit there is *someone* who has been paying me a little attention lately."

B.J. thought he could guess who. "Straws Monahan, right?" The successful horseman had been widowed for almost as many years as Olive. "He was asking about you the other day."

His mother started. "Straws?" She got up from her stool, closing the laptop. "Really, B.J. That's the most ridiculous idea I've ever heard."

As she walked out of the room, B.J. was left there wondering. If it wasn't Straws, then who did his mother have her eye on?

Saturday Savannah had a list of chores to do in town, beginning with a visit with her mother. She took Francine for a walk along the gravel path on the bank of Coffee Creek and listened while she prattled about characters and plotlines from her favorite movies. Francine's only moment of lucidity came when she asked about her flower garden.

Foreseeing this question, Savannah had brought along an iPad with at least a dozen photos. The transformation in her mother was startling. "The heliopsis needs pinching back and the roses should be deadheaded and dusted for aphids. A little extra mulching material wouldn't hurt, either. There's a wood chipper in the shed. See if it still works."

"Okay." Savannah stared at her mother, amazed. "You must really miss gardening."

Francine nodded.

"Would you like to come home this afternoon? You could help me with the deadheading and pinching back and show me how to use the mulcher."

"Oh. I don't know. The farm is a long way from here."

Francine's voice trailed off and she grew quiet, not responding to Savannah's next few questions. By the time they had turned back for the home she'd started muttering to herself, and Savannah was forced to concede that her mother's moment of clarity was over.

Once Francine had been settled in the dining room for morning coffee and snacks, Savannah headed to Molly's Market to restock on frozen entrées, coffee and bread for her morning toast. Her grocery cart looked as if it belonged to a student, not a grown-up, Savannah thought ruefully.

Without Regan at home, it just didn't seem worth the effort to prepare regular meals. Savannah sighed as she moved down the next aisle. She'd got through her errands faster than usual, and suddenly she realized why.

Most weeks when she shopped for her provisions she was stopped several times by citizens who wanted to tell her something or ask a question.

Today, however, despite the fact that the store was busy, no one had said a word to her.

Not even in the checkout line.

But they did look at her. She caught discreet glances and heard whispers, but when she turned, heads were averted and eye contact avoided.

Savannah's face heated up as she realized the probable explanation. The news about the unknown traveler's body being exhumed must be widely known by now. People would be talking about what had happened the night he was found—and remembering that her brother had been there. Maybe word had spread about B.J. kissing her in Monahan's parking lot, too.

She'd sure given the town lots to gossip about.

Savannah pushed her cart forward and began unloading her groceries. Molly's husband was at the till this morning. Usually Al was a bit of a jokester, but today he silently took her money and returned the change to her outstretched palm. Was it her imagination, or had he been extra careful not to come into contact with her skin?

Savannah struggled to hold her head high and keep her expression neutral as she carried her bags of groceries to the SUV. Her next stop, at the Cinnamon Stick for coffee, was much the same. She would swear the table of older women at the back corner were whispering about her. Even pretty little Dawn Dolan gave her a strange look before filling up her take-out mug.

As she crossed Main Street for her SUV, Savannah felt as if she was fifteen years old again, walking the length of the high school cafeteria, trying to pretend she didn't hear the other kids gossiping about her drunken father and crazy mother.

At least back then she'd had the support of B.J. and his friends, who had stood by her and Hunter, scoffing and belittling those who wanted to put the new Moody kids in their place.

But today she was alone, and even though she was an adult, it hurt to see how quickly the community she'd thought she was an integral member of could turn against her.

In the SUV, doors and windows closed tight, engine running to provide air-conditioning against the day's rising heat, she pulled out her phone and dialed B.J.

"Hey, Savannah." He sounded as though he was in a good mood and happy to hear from her.

He wouldn't be either soon.

"Have you been to town today?"

"Uh, sure." He sounded taken aback by her curt tone.

"Where did you go?"

"I picked up an order from Ed's, gassed up my truck and stopped for a coffee and cinnamon bun. Why?"

"How were you treated?"

"That's a crazy question. Savannah, what's going on?"

"Just answer me, please. The people in the stores, the other customers, passersby… Were they friendly? Did they talk to you?"

"Of course they talked to me. This is Coffee Creek."

"More importantly, you're Bob and Olive Lambert's son."

Family mattered in Coffee Creek. No matter how good a job she did, no one would ever forget where she'd come from. She pressed the heel of her hand to her forehead. She could feel the beginning of a headache coming on.

"What the hell do my parents have to do with it?"

"Never mind, B.J. You wouldn't understand."

She ended the call, powered off her phone and then drove out of town trying to pretend she didn't care about any of this.

But it wasn't true.

Without the support of her own town, she'd never get reelected.

As she was carrying her purchases in through the front door, a business card fell to the worn wood floor. Savannah set the bags down first then went back to retrieve it.

It was a calling card from the Realtor's office in Lewistown. The same one that had contacted her earlier about possibly selling her property. Before her mother had moved into the care home, Francine had gone to the lawyer's office and signed papers giving Savannah the right to act as her executor.

So the decision was all Savannah's to make.

She stared at the card, thinking. She'd been considering selling to come up with the money for Regan to go to medical school. But maybe this was an opportunity for an even bigger change. She could sell their home and the land and move to a new community where she and her mom could make a fresh start. She'd set aside a fair share of the money for Hunter, as well. Maybe he could go back to school and learn a trade.

Something a little steadier than being a rodeo cowboy.

Another rodeo cowboy came to mind then. It didn't matter how far she moved—she'd never forget B.J.

But she could try.

B.J. was under no illusions. He knew Savannah didn't want to see him. But he couldn't stay away.

Besides, he was bored.

The whole damn family had plans this Sunday that didn't involve him.

Cassidy had informed him in no uncertain terms that she and Farley had a quiet romantic evening planned. And Jackson had moved his belongings to Maddie Turner's spread today and was spending the evening with her. B.J.'s mother was out at a meeting, planning for the construction of a historical site at the intersection of Highway 81 and Main Street. And Corb, Laurel and Stephanie had gone to Highwood to visit Winnie Hays and her new baby.

Olive had cocked her head when she'd heard this news. So far she hadn't been invited to see her new grandson. It was her own damn fault, of course. If she'd been nicer to Winnie in the beginning, things might have been different.

But Olive couldn't see that. In her mind, her daughter-in-law was just being unreasonable by staying in Highwood and not returning to Coffee Creek.

B.J. wandered around the empty house, then went out on the deck to take in the view.

For the first time in many years he was home—and content to be here.

He'd done a lot of traveling in this country. If a town had a PRCA-sponsored rodeo, he'd probably been there. As a result he'd seen a lot of Mother Nature at her finest. He especially loved the mountains and red canyons of New Mexico, Utah and Wyoming.

But on an evening like this, when the sky was stretched out above him, snow-topped mountains lining the horizon and fields of grazing pastures and hay undulating in every direction, he couldn't imagine any place in the world that had more to offer than Montana.

Something strange was happening to him.

He'd noticed it yesterday, when he was working in the barn with Farley.

A deep sense of belonging and contentment had washed over him. After so many years of traveling the circuit he had finally committed to one place, and it felt good.

Life wasn't perfect on Coffee Creek Ranch. But it was home. Strange to think it had taken him so many years to realize it.

He'd spoken to Jackson just this morning about the final transition.

"You sure you're doing the right thing? You know you'll always be welcome to come back."

"I won't change my mind." Jackson had clasped a hand to his shoulder. "I just hope you don't feel you've been railroaded into settling on the family ranch?"

"I don't." B.J. would have said as much to make Jackson feel better. But the funny thing was—it was true.

And something else was crystal clear, too.

He and Savannah were soul mates.

He didn't consider himself a romantic guy,

and he certainly wasn't touchy-feely with his emotions.

But there were no other words to explain the connection he felt to her.

And maybe she wanted space right now, but to him, being apart wasn't the answer. They'd been apart eighteen years.

And he was done with that.

With a renewed sense of purpose, B.J. got into his truck and drove a mile past the turn-off to the town of Coffee Creek, then hung a right onto the graveled road that led to the Moodys' acreage. Savannah's SUV was parked in what he now recognized as its usual spot. He drove in behind it, leaving his keys in the ignition as he gathered his courage to face her again.

He was pretty sure she was going to ask him to leave.

And he didn't think the bouquet of sweet peas he'd brought from his mother's garden was going to change her mind.

But the flowers couldn't hurt, right?

Since the evening was warm and there were still a few hours before dark, he'd expected to find her on the porch. But all he saw were the plastic-tray remains of a frozen dinner and an empty bottle of beer.

Good Lord, how did she survive on such

a lousy diet? Even when he was on the road, he'd eaten better than she.

He knocked on the front door, and when there was no answer, wandered around to the back.

She'd done some handiwork since his last visit. The window frames were freshly painted. The screen door had been repaired.

It crossed his mind that he should go inside and make sure nothing bad had happened to her. Both the front and back doors were unlocked—he'd checked.

But he decided to try one more spot first.

Last time he'd been here, to tow away those old junk heaps, he'd mowed a bunch of the wild grass growing around the property. It looked as though Savannah had carried on with the job. Back of the house a larger swath of property had recently been cut. He followed the path of the mower and eventually found himself on the knoll looking over the valley.

And there she was. Sitting on the grass, in a pair of grass-stained shorts, looking out at her million-dollar view. On her white T-shirt were streaks of the blue paint she'd used on the window frames.

"You again." Her tone was surprisingly mild.

"Yup." The mower—probably out of gas by

now—was in his path. He stepped around it, then went to sit beside her.

"I brought you some flowers. But they seem pretty insignificant compared to everything around us."

She surprised him again by taking them out of his hands and inhaling the fragrance. "I love sweet peas."

Score one for his side.

"I'm glad. I wasn't sure what my reception would be like. I almost expected you to draw your weapon."

"I might have. But it's locked away in the house."

Despite the warm evening, Savannah shivered. Would she always feel this secret thrill every time he sneaked up on her?

The attraction was about more than his dark-haired good looks and his tough, cowboy-fit body. Something sizzled between them as she looked into his dark gray eyes.

She drew up her knees and hugged them, resting her cheek so she was facing him. He was wearing a gray T-shirt that defined his broad shoulders and chest and the tapering thinness of his waist. Not a pound to spare on this rodeo cowboy.

"You've been busy." He touched a grass

stain on her shorts, then a botch of paint on the hem of her T-shirt. "Still fixing up the place?"

She sighed. "It's what you do when you're trying to sell."

He blinked. "Has Regan been accepted to medical school, then?"

"Not yet. But I'm going to sell anyway. Move to another town. Start over."

His body tensed and his eyes narrowed. "Is this about that strange conversation we had on the phone today?"

"Partly."

"You better tell me exactly what happened."

She'd been holding in the anger and hurt all weekend. Now it was a relief to be asked to spill it all out. "I went in to get groceries and a coffee at the Cinnamon Stick yesterday. No one would talk to me. They acted like I'd just arrived from another planet."

"Seriously?"

"I'm sure the townspeople were already uneasy with June Savage nosing around and asking all her questions. Now that the body's been exhumed, it's getting more serious. Last election most people had forgotten about the old barn burning down. Now everyone is remembering—and wondering why they elected a sheriff whose brother may have had something to do with a young man's death."

"That's crazy. People don't think that way about you."

He sounded sincere. But he hadn't been there. "You wouldn't say that if you had seen how I was treated yesterday."

"I just wish I had." He clenched his fists.

Savannah reached over to cover his hand with one of hers. "That isn't the answer."

He twisted his wrists and suddenly *he* was the one holding *her* hand. "And you think leaving town is?"

"I'm up for reelection next November, and I'd say my chances of a second term are next to zero. I don't know if I can handle that."

"You're jumping to conclusions. One bad day isn't going to undo all the years of good work you've given this county."

"I wish I could believe that." She didn't think B.J. could understand what it was like for her, not when he came from a respectable, upstanding family like the Lamberts. His father had been one of Sheriff Smith's best friends.

Her father had been an inmate more than once, in Sheriff Smith's detention cell.

"Even if you aren't reelected, you could always get another job. I know we'd be glad to hire you at Coffee Creek Ranch."

"I don't have a clue about cattle or horses."

"You could learn."

She shook her head. He didn't understand how wonderful it felt to walk the streets in her uniform, or to patrol the highways in her SUV, knowing she was someone people could look up to and respect. She'd never had that in her life before her career in law enforcement.

"It won't come to that, anyway. You'll be elected again because you're a good sheriff. And a damn sexy one, besides."

"You know all the smooth lines."

"I only say them because they're true."

He touched her face, a soft stroke that made her feel cherished—a novel experience for her. Then he put his hand on her shoulder and pulled her next to him.

She leaned her weight against his chest, and he tightened his hold. She could feel him resting his face against the top of her head.

"Your hair smells like grass cuttings and fresh air...with a faint undertone of paint."

"It's my signature scent."

He chuckled. Then tipped her chin upward so he could see her eyes. "We've got to stop fighting each other. We're on the same side."

Then he kissed her, softly and slowly. Tasting first her lips, then deepening the kiss and pulling her down to the earth, where their bodies tangled together.

After a long while, she drew away from him. "You keep tempting me. And I keep giving in. But I'm afraid it's a mistake."

"It isn't. It can't be."

"But it won't look right. The people in this town—"

"Don't matter," he said, finishing her sentence for her. "You think I care what Ed at the feed supply store or Molly at the market thinks about you? I damn well don't. And you shouldn't, either."

She sighed, taking a finger and tracing the line of his jaw to the tip of his chin. "But I need Ed at the feed supply store and Molly at the market to vote for me."

He groaned. "Do you really think they care who you're sleeping with?"

"I—" When he put it that way, she didn't.

"Now, can I make love to you here? Or would you prefer a bed?"

She laughed. "Those are my only two options, are they?"

"Sweetheart, I've waited over half my life to make love with you. But I'm damn well not waiting another day."

Chapter 12

Savannah's bedroom was plain in the extreme. Sheer white curtains billowed at the open window. A double bed, unmade and yet not untidy, had crisp white sheets and a thin, pale blue comforter.

B.J. noticed the neon glare of the alarm clock: 7:45 p.m.

A beaten-up cowboy hat and her sheriff's star sat on a sea-green dresser.

And then he was done looking at anything but the sexiest woman he'd ever known. He tangled his hands in her thick, long hair and studied her smoky, sultry eyes. "God, you drive me wild, woman."

She placed her hands on either side of his neck. "Is that so, cowboy?"

She had no idea how much he wanted her. He had years and years of pent-up desire surging through his bloodstream right now. But more important than any of that was making her feel cherished and special. Letting her know that his commitment to her was true and forever.

He kissed her, deeply and passionately, running his hands down her strong, slender back, then finding the hem of her shirt and working it upward.

She wiggled free of the paint-stained cotton, and her bra was next, coming undone with a quick twist then falling to the floor with the shirt.

She had beautiful breasts, the same toffee color as the rest of her skin. He had to feel them, kiss them, admire them, before moving on to her shorts, undoing the snap and inching the denim fabric over her luscious hips.

"Your turn, cowboy."

Her body was such a temptation, he could hardly endure the wait as she pulled at his jeans, then slid her hands under his cotton T-shirt. "You look so sexy in this," she said, but still she pulled it off, over his head. "But even better without it."

He'd never been so aroused, but he laid her on the bed with the intention of loving every inch of her body before he even thought of himself.

He was finally in her bed.

The evening was young.

And he was determined to make it one she'd never forget.

Savannah had known she was taking a big step when she invited B.J. into her bedroom. She hadn't realized it would change her world. She'd never felt so much—of anything. Physical, mind-bending pleasure, beyond what she had imagined.

But also a transformative connection that existed on another plane. Looking into B.J.'s eyes, she felt as if she was seeing the future.

Their arms and legs were still tangled together, minus the top sheet and comforter, which were somewhere on the floor. She had her hand on his bare chest and could feel the thumping of his heart.

The night had been long, most of it spent in bed. There had been a sojourn to the kitchen for snacks and water.

Then back to bed.

Now it was so late, she was afraid to look at her clock.

"Are you happy?" B.J. asked.

"Yes." Happier than she'd ever been in her life. But she didn't tell him that. She trusted him. But not enough to put her open heart entirely in his hands.

"Good. Me, too." He gave her a charming half smile. "I'm pretty tired, as well."

"No wonder."

He laughed at her dry tone. "Close your eyes, sweetheart."

"You're staying the night?" She hadn't expected that. But then, she hadn't thought very far into the future about anything to do with their relationship.

"It's almost over. Might as well stay put for the last few hours. Unless you want me to leave?"

"No." Her eyes fluttered closed as she gave in to the fatigue washing over her. He smoothed down her hair. His touch felt gentle and loving. That was her last thought before she drifted off.

An obnoxious sound woke her. It could have been hours later; it could have been an entire day. She sprang upright in her bed, noticing B.J. sprawled out beside her, eyes still closed.

Then the sound rang out again and she realized it was her cell phone.

"Damn!" She peeled B.J.'s arm off her leg and grabbed the phone from the table by her bed. The cheerful bright numbers on her alarm clock informed her that it was five minutes past nine.

She *never* slept this late. Especially not on a workday.

"Sheriff Moody here."

"Hey, Savannah? Are you sick or something?"

It was her dispatcher, Haley, on the line.

"No—I was just held up this morning."

"Oh." Haley waited a beat, then continued, "A state attorney just called."

"Paul Corrigan?"

"That's the guy. Didn't you and he—"

"Ancient history, Haley." Savannah was quick to sidestep the inquisition. "What did he want?"

"Just to tell you the dental records were a match."

She'd been expecting as much. Still, she experienced a queer feeling in her gut. "Has the family been notified?"

"Yes. June Savage is making arrangements for the remains to be returned to their family burial plot."

"Good. Thanks, Haley. I'll be in soon as I can."

"I take it that was bad news?" B.J.'s voice was gravelly. He'd propped himself up in the bed, and his eyes were already sharp and focused, as if he'd been awake for hours.

"Depends on your outlook, I guess. Bad news for the McBrides. The dental records matched."

B.J. looked at her in silence for several seconds. "Well, at least his family doesn't have to live with uncertainty anymore."

"Yes, but they don't have the hope he could be alive, either."

Their conversation was interrupted by a second phone call, this one from Paul himself.

"Looks like we're reopening the investigation. The guy in charge is Rex Harris. You know him?"

"Yes." She wished she didn't. The few times they'd had business together, Rex—who was in his late forties and something of a throwback where rednecks were concerned—had treated her as if she was a little girl. Real nice, but real condescending, too.

"He's going to come 'round to pick up your files."

Savannah rolled her eyes, thinking of the

slim folder that held the sum total of Sheriff Smith's investigation.

"And I imagine his next step will be tracking down your brother for questioning. And that Lambert fellow."

Thank God Paul didn't know that "Lambert fellow" was just now getting out of her bed and pulling on his clothes. "Thanks for the heads-up, Paul.

"And tell Rex good luck in finding my brother," she added.

But locating Hunter was easier than Savannah had expected. She was just out of the shower when she heard the sound of male voices coming from the kitchen.

B.J. had promised to brew some coffee and make her toast before he left. Did he have a habit of talking to himself while he cooked?

She slipped from the bathroom to her adjoining bedroom, where she dressed in clean jeans, her short-sleeved tan shirt and her belt. As a last step she pinned on her star.

She was finger-combing her damp hair when she walked into the kitchen, only to stop cold at the sight of Hunter at the kitchen table, B.J. sitting opposite.

"Hey, sis." Hunter got up to give her a hug, made awkward by the cast on his left arm.

He seemed thinner than ever, and he had a fresh scar above one of his eyebrows. Despite these injuries, her brother still had his same cocky grin.

"What happened? Are you okay?"

"Depends on your definition. Am I going to live? Yes. Am I going to be able to compete for the next two weeks? No."

"When did this happen?" She pointed to the cast.

"About a month ago."

"Is that why you didn't show up for the Wild Rogue?"

"Yeah—but how did you know about that?"

She could tell him she'd driven all that way for the chance to spend some time with him. But why bother? "Never mind about that. What brings you home? Need some recovery time?"

"That's part of it."

Hunter sat down again, and picked a slice of toast off the pile at the center of the table. "B.J. was just filling me in on a few local events. First and foremost is the fact that you two are finally back together. Sure took you long enough."

She glanced at B.J., who winked then came up beside her.

"You look like you need this." He handed

her a mug of coffee. "And this." He gave her a nice, sweet kiss, right in front of her brother.

"That's what I'm talking about." Hunter hooted. "So when did you two finally figure out you belonged together?"

"Hang on a minute. You don't get to ask the questions here." Darn her brother and his timing. This day had started out crazy and seemed to be getting more insane by the minute. "What happened to your arm?"

"I'll give you three guesses and one clue. It had something to do with a bull."

"Hunter, no! You promised no more bulls." All rodeo events were potentially dangerous. But bull riding was the worst.

"I didn't exactly *promise*."

She shook her head. She hadn't been able to control her brother when they were growing up, so what made her think he would listen to her now that they were in their thirties?

"It was a hell of a ride, though. You can see the video on YouTube. Got a computer handy?" Hunter was already edging out of his chair. She motioned for him to sit back down.

"I *don't* want to watch footage of you getting hurt. Really, Hunter. How much longer are you planning to live this lifestyle?"

She might have asked B.J. the same question a few weeks ago. But it seemed as if he had finally decided to settle down on his family's ranch. What would it take to pull her brother out of the dangerous rodeo-circuit lifestyle?

"I'm going to keep doing what I'm doing as long as it pays the bills. Soon as this arm is healed, I'll be on my way. But I was hoping I could crash here for a few weeks?"

"Of course. It's your home as much as it is mine." Later she would talk to him about her plans to sell the place. She had no doubt that Hunter would agree—as long as he could pocket his share of the cash. She'd use her own share to ensure quality care for their mother for the rest of her life.

This was all assuming Hunter didn't end up in serious legal trouble.

"I'm sorry about your arm. But your timing is good. I was just going to send another email asking you to come home."

Hunter drummed his fingers on the table. He'd never been able to sit still for long. "Yeah, I saw your messages."

She stared at him. So why hadn't he answered?

And then it occurred to her that he'd probably been talking to someone else in Coffee Creek.

"Did Hanna White ask you to come back?"

Hunter's smile lost its cocky edge. He fingered the rim of his coffee cup and gave a slight nod.

"So she told you that they've figured out who the man that died in the fire was?"

He lifted his head slightly, directing narrowed eyes at her in a cautious glance. "She said it wasn't confirmed yet, but he might be the son of some rich bastard from L.A."

"As of today you can consider it confirmed. His name was Travis McBride. Did you know him, Hunter?"

Her brother didn't answer, just fidgeted with his coffee cup.

B.J. pulled his chair closer to Hunter and leaned in toward him. "It's going to be okay, as long as we're clear about what happened. We were in the barn when the lightning struck, but we had no idea there was anyone in the loft. Then we took off as fast as we could to report the fire."

Savannah felt sick to her stomach. B.J. was obviously coaching her brother on what to say. Right in front of her! But she was the sheriff. It was her responsibility to find out the truth. Even when the case involved her brother and the man she loved.

She turned to pour her coffee down the drain, more shaken than she wanted either man to see. Not just by B.J.'s blatant attempt to collude with Hunter.

But also by her feelings.

She loved B.J. It was the first time she'd admitted this to herself.

But it had been true a lot longer. She was staring out the window over the sink when she heard her brother say to B.J., "You prepared to swear on that?"

"I'll give your sister a signed statement, right now."

"Better give it to Rex Harris. He's the man heading the investigation." Her voice sounded leaden, even to her own ears.

How had the best night of his life morphed into one of the worst mornings ever?

B.J. didn't make it back to Coffee Creek until shortly after ten. Jay and Griff had already done the morning chores and were out checking fences in the northwest pasture. B.J. went to the office to get a handle on the week's schedule. He found his mother there, pacing the floor and looking annoyed.

"I admit when you first told me that you were ready to come back to the ranch, I was thrilled. But I expected you to take the job seriously. Corb and I and the other hands start our day at six in the morning. Not ten-fif-teen." She glanced, pointedly, at her watch.

B.J. had been afraid of this—micromanag-ing by his mother was definitely one of the hazards of coming back home.

"I appreciate that, Mom. But we've got a schedule here." He pointed to one of several whiteboards hanging on the wall. "The boys and I rotate so we each get two mornings off per week and one full day. You can see here that Monday and Wednesday are my off mornings."

Olive furrowed her brow as she studied the schedule. Then she relented, a little. "Well, that's fine and good, but I still think you should be watching where you spend your time. There's lots of talk going around the community—about you and our sheriff."

"They can talk all they want, Mom. It won't change anything—least of all the way I feel about Savannah."

He could tell Olive didn't care for his re-sponse. "You don't like making things easy for yourself, do you, son? Can't you see how bad it looks? Especially since they've re-opened that accidental-death case from when you were a boy. Everyone's going to say that you and Hunter were in it together."

"Well, we were, Mom."

Her frown sharpened. "You were there that night. But you had nothing to do with that young man being up in the loft."

Here it was, the first real test of his resolve. B.J. kept a lot of things from his mother, but he wasn't fond of actually lying to her.

But he needed to protect Savannah. And that meant protecting her brother.

And it started here and now.

"Neither did Hunter."

"You're only saying that because you want to protect him. This is serious, B.J. Your feelings for that woman are going to ruin your life."

"That's what you want to believe. But I'm not perfect, Mom. I've made mistakes—big ones—in my life. And I happen to believe I'm not the only Lambert who's done so."

His mother narrowed her eyes. "And what's that supposed to mean?"

"You haven't spoken to your own sister for over thirty years. What's up with that? I've met her. She's not perfect—none of us are—but she's family, right? And didn't you and Dad raise us to believe that family comes first?"

"Stop it right there, Robert. You don't understand the first thing about my childhood, or the issues I had with my sister."

"Well, why don't you tell me, then? What's the big secret?"

"It is no secret. I've already told Corb and I'm sure he told you that my sister prevented me from visiting my father after he had his stroke. He died and I never even had the chance to say goodbye."

"I know that's what you told Corb. But is it really why you've stayed so angry all these years? Isn't it possible that you're really mad because your father blamed you for your mother's death?"

His mother gasped. "Did Maddie tell you that?"

"Not in so many words. But I guessed from looking at the family photos. If it *was* true, then it was cruel and unfair of Grandpa Turner—but it wasn't Maddie's fault. I've met her, Mom. She's not a bad person."

His mother held out her hand. "Stop," she said again. "I refuse to discuss this with you any further. I'm beginning to wish you'd stayed on the rodeo circuit. I never thought a son of mine would be so vicious."

She was gone by the time B.J. had cooled down enough to realize that he'd pushed too far. He'd wanted to get her to back off on bad-mouthing Savannah and her family. But he shouldn't have lashed out in return. His parents hadn't been perfect, but they'd loved him.

B.J. thought about following his mother and apologizing, but he had a meeting scheduled in fifteen minutes. A woman was applying to be the agent and office manager—responsible for keeping the quarter-horse records current, updating their website and handling daily correspondence. This was all work that Brock and Jackson had previously handled and had been sorely neglected in the past few months.

Once the interview had been concluded, B.J. promised to call the woman back shortly with his decision. He'd been impressed with her experience and her knowledge about quarter horses. She'd be a great addition to the business, as long as her references checked out.

Now it was time to apologize to his mother.

He found her just about to get into her SUV. She was dressed in a pair of slacks and a blazer, all made-up with her hair perfectly in place.

"Mom? Do you have a minute?"

"I'm on my way to a meeting of the historical-site committee. Work is starting this week and I want to make sure they follow our plans to the letter."

She sounded like her normal self, only her voice was brittle and she wore sunglasses so he couldn't read her expression.

"Well, I won't keep you. But I did want to say that I'm sorry for what I said earlier."

"I've already forgiven you, son. I know you felt I had no right to say those things about Savannah and you were just lashing out. But I appreciate the apology."

Standing alone by the big SUV, she looked so small and defenseless that he felt even worse for the things he'd said.

"That's no excuse for me being a jerk. Sometimes I don't think I fully appreciate how lucky I was to have a mother and father like you and Dad. You gave us kids everything we needed and a whole lot more."

It was part of what set him apart from Savannah. She always claimed that he couldn't know what it was like to grow up with parents who couldn't take care of themselves, let alone their children. And the older he got, the more he realized how much difference that made.

"It's good to hear you say that."

He moved closer. "I'd give you a hug but you're all dressed up."

"A kiss would be nice." She turned her cheek to him and he gave her a warm peck.

"I love you, Mom."

"You're a good son, B.J. I love you, too, and I'm very proud of you."

Watching her drive off, B.J. wondered if she'd still feel that way after he'd made his official statement to the new investigator.

Chapter 13

Some cattle were missing from the Bar K Ranch east of Coffee Creek, and Savannah was actually happy to field the call. She couldn't have coped with sitting around in the office today doing paperwork when she had so many worries on her mind.

Number one was Hunter. She'd arranged a meeting for him with a defense attorney in Lewistown, and he'd set off in his truck half an hour ago. She'd wanted to go with him, but he'd brushed that offer away, telling her that he was picking up Hanna White and she would be with him for moral support.

"Not much you could do for me, anyway," he'd said. "Like B.J. said this morning, all I have to do is tell the truth, stick to the facts and not embellish anything."

The "not embellishing" part would be difficult for Hunter. But Savannah could only go so far to protect her brother. If he chose to have Hanna by his side, instead of his sister, that was his decision to make.

Besides, her regard for Hanna was growing. She was certainly impressed that Hanna had been able to convince Hunter to come home. Facing the music had never been his strong suit before.

Savannah arrived at the Bar K an hour after they'd made their call, and she could tell middle-aged rancher Wade Kincaid was impressed.

"You made good time."

"I don't like the idea of a cow rustler moving into our county. You say you're missing four yearlings?" The barbed-wire fence had been cut and she could see tire tracks right up to the opening.

"Yup. I figure he loaded them up there." He pointed to the break in the fence. Just beyond the gap, about twenty Black Angus, some with spring calves, were watching curiously.

"Branded?"

"You bet."

She took pictures of the crime scene and

made molds of the tire tracks. Then she went up to one of the cows and got a picture of the brand. All the while Wade watched thoughtfully.

She wondered if he'd heard any of the local gossip. Hopefully if she did a good job here, he would disregard it if he had.

"Those tracks were fresh," she said. "The cattle were probably stolen last night. You just noticed them missing this morning?"

"Yeah. Ruby and I were out checking fences." He nodded at a stunning bloodred bay tied to a tree on the other side of the fence. "Never expected to run into this sort of trouble."

Savannah pulled out the paperwork next, guiding Wade through the forms, then getting his signature.

"We'll put this in the database and alert the sale barns. But I'll also be checking with your neighbors to see if anyone noticed strange vehicles on the road and also to warn them to watch their own herds."

Once their business was wrapped up, Wade shook her hand and his parting words confirmed her worst fears. "I don't care what anyone says, you do a damn fine job. Keep up the good work."

* * *

I don't care what anyone says. Wade's words stayed with Savannah all day long. They were eerily similar to what B.J. had said to her not twenty-four hours earlier.

But it was easy for them to say, wasn't it? No one was questioning whether Wade Kincaid was a good rancher or B. J. Lambert a good cowboy.

She was the one under the microscope here. Always had been. Always would be.

Part of it was the nature of her job. She could have kept on as a deputy sheriff. Getting reelected wouldn't be an issue then.

But she'd wanted the job precisely because of the respectability that came with it. Only maybe she'd been kidding herself. If people were already talking about her, how much respect had she had in the first place?

Savannah worked through lunch, taking only a ten-minute break to get her mail. Burt Snow, the postmaster, gave her a curious look but didn't say much other than hello. Burt was a quiet, middle-aged man who generally kept to himself, especially since his divorce a few years ago from Tabitha, the librarian.

Savannah pulled a flyer, a letter from the University of Oregon and a postcard out of her slot.

She turned over the letter from the university a few times. Her sister had given her permission to look at anything related to her med-school applications. She took a deep breath and opened the envelope.

We regret to inform you...

Damn. This was the second rejection this summer.

She read the postcard from Washington next.

Having so much fun. Our capital is unbelievable!

Maybe Regan had been smart to go on this trip, after all. She only had one school left to hear from. What were the odds the news would be positive?

Savannah, who usually had so much faith in her little sister's abilities, couldn't find it in herself to be hopeful anymore.

She said goodbye to Burt, then went back to her office. At one-thirty Haley brought her a sandwich—the daily special from the Cinnamon Stick.

"You need to eat, boss."

"Thanks." She barely lifted her head from her paperwork. "Heard anything about those stolen yearlings?"

"Not yet."

She could sense Haley waiting, as if she had something else to talk about. "Any calls from Paul Corrigan or the state investigator?"

Haley shook her head. "What's going to happen with that? Is it true that they might try your brother and B. J. Lambert for mitigated homicide?"

Oh, hell. Here it was. The gossip had even infiltrated her own office.

"It's out of my hands. But I can't see them having enough evidence for that."

It was true. The evidence was paltry. But still, she would have appreciated a call from Paul or Rex Harris to keep her in the loop. She was longing to check in with her brother, as well, but since he didn't have a cell phone, she supposed she'd have to wait until later that night.

Assuming he came home, that was.

B.J. called her around five. She had to admit it was nice to hear his voice.

"Let's go out on a real date," he suggested.

She was tempted. "On a Monday night?"

"All the better. The restaurants won't be busy and we'll get in without a reservation."

"Very funny. The Green Verandah doesn't even take reservations."

"I was thinking we'd go to Lewistown."

She was touched that he wanted to take her someplace special. But it wasn't a good idea. "I need to stick close to home tonight. I'm hoping to find out how things went for Hunter with the lawyer."

B.J. hesitated, then said, "Fair enough. Green Verandah it is. Can I pick you up at seven?"

Savannah did some quick math. She needed time to visit her mom for half an hour, then go home and shower and get ready. For a change, she wanted to dress up a little. Wear a pretty sundress and even shoes with a heel.

"Seven would be fine."

The sheriff badge and cowboy hat would be staying home tonight. She might even blow-dry her hair.

"Wow, wow and wow."

B.J.'s reaction was everything she could have hoped for. Savannah came down the stairs from the porch as soon as she heard his truck. He was already in her yard, waiting for her, and he placed his hands on her shoulders as he kissed her hello.

Then took a moment for his eyes to tell her just how much he liked her new look.

"I can't remember the last time I saw you in a dress."

"High school graduation?" They'd both gone without a date, since they'd broken up two months previously. Savannah remembered it as a colorless night. She'd still been pretty devastated, as Hunter had only recently run off to the rodeo.

Days after the ceremony and dance, B.J. had left town for his first rodeo, too.

After that, she'd seen him rarely.

"That's not a great memory for me," B.J. said.

"Me, either."

"Hopefully we can start making some better ones now that we're together again." He gave her a smile that made her heart do a happy dance. This was the best she'd felt all day. With B.J. by her side, none of her problems seemed insurmountable.

At the Green Verandah they sat outside in wicker chairs and ordered the basket of ribs to share, with coleslaw on the side, rather than fries.

"I love these long summer evenings. It's fun people-watching." Just checking out the traffic in and out of the Lonesome Spur Saloon across the street was worth the price of the dinner, Savannah thought.

"The only person I want to watch is sitting right across from me." B.J. placed his hand over hers. "I lost my cool with my mother today."

"Was she upset that you spent the night at my place?"

"Yeah. Then I went on the offensive and tore into Mom for being estranged from her sister for so long."

He'd talked about his aunt Maddie quite a bit last night. Savannah knew he felt guilty that she was suffering with lung cancer without the support of her extended family.

"Maybe it isn't all her fault."

"But I get the feeling Maddie would be open to a reconciliation. If I sensed the same thing in my mother, I could maybe organize something."

"I don't know. You'd better stay out of it." Savannah rolled her eyes when she realized what she'd said. "But then, who am I to give advice? According to Hunter and Regan, I'm always butting in when it's not my business."

"We're both the oldest child in our families. I think it's how we were programmed."

He was probably right about that. And for the most part, she liked B.J.'s take-charge attitude. She could never be with a man who was too easygoing. No matter how hard she tried not to, she'd just end up walking all over him.

"There's something else I need to tell you about my day," B.J. said.

"That sounds ominous."

"This afternoon I had a visit from Rex Harris."

She tensed. The state investigator wasn't wasting any time with this. "Did he want a statement?"

B.J. nodded. "I told him pretty much word for word what I said in your kitchen that morning."

Savannah didn't know what to say. She was almost positive that B.J. was lying to protect Hunter. But if he told the truth—how much trouble would Hunter be in?

"Did he seem to believe you?" she finally asked.

B.J.'s jaw tightened. "Not sure. There were a lot of questions about the watch. He tried to catch me out by describing it as gold one time and silver the next. I guess he wanted to see if I would jump in to correct him. Of course that didn't work, since I have no idea what the bloody thing looks like."

Score one for B.J. Would her brother pass that test, too? If she could just find him tonight, she'd be able to warn him what to expect when he was questioned—unless Rex Harris had already interviewed him, as well?

She hated being in the dark like this.

Hated even more not knowing what had *really* happened.

She wanted to believe the facts as B.J. had outlined them that morning. But her sixth sense—the one all good investigators had—wouldn't buy it.

"Did he ask you anything else?"

"Just to account for every minute of that day, again implying that I had met Travis somewhere and then lured him out to a remote location so I could get him drunk and rob him."

She sighed and shook her head. "This is so crazy." Yet, she could see why Rex had come up with that theory—it explained a lot of questions that were currently unanswered.

Savannah, by instinct keeping an eye on the street and the saloon across the way, noticed a familiar black truck turning off the highway onto Main Street and heading their way. Within seconds she recognized it as Hunter's. He parked outside the Lonesome Spur Saloon and both he and Hanna White got out of the cab.

Neither of them noticed her and B.J. sitting almost a hundred yards away at their outside table. They were too busy arguing. At one point Hanna put both her hands on Hunter's chest and gave him a shove. Their voices kept rising, to the point where their words could finally be understood.

"...so forget it!" Hunter yelled.

"Don't worry. I will!" Hanna stomped off then, heading in the direction of the home she rented on Fir Lane. Hunter stared after her for a moment, fists balled up, but arms hanging limply at his sides. Then he swore and headed for the saloon, looking as if he needed a double—and a designated driver to see him safely home.

Savannah was out of her seat before she realized she was still on a date.

B.J. raised his eyebrows. "Was it something I said?"

"Funny guy. Do you mind if I go find out what happened?"

"Being that bossy older sister again, are you?" His smile took the edge off the words.

"Maybe. Some combination of that and being the local sheriff. I really am sorry to bust up this date, though. I was having a good time."

"Me, too. And I'm not ready for it to end. Why don't you go ahead. I'll settle up here and meet you at the saloon in a few."

She thanked him with a quick kiss, then grabbed her purse—something she wasn't used to having with her and was worried about forgetting—and headed across the street.

First she wanted to talk to Hanna, before she disappeared from sight. The other woman was walking as fast as she could, but her heels and narrow skirt were slowing her down. Still, Savannah had to jog to catch up to her. Not an easy feat since she, too, was wearing heels.

"Hanna! Can I speak to you a minute, please?"

The other woman cast her a suspicious look. "Are you asking as the sheriff? Or Hunter's older sister?"

She thought about that. "His sister."

"Well, then. Let me get something off my mind." Hanna put her hands on her hips, her suddenly offensive stance belying the feminine outfit she was wearing. "I know you never liked me. You didn't think I was good enough for your brother. What a laugh! *He's the one* who isn't good enough for *me!*"

"You're probably right about that."

"No kidding I'm right. Foolish me to wait all these years while he was having fun on the rodeo circuit. I thought he'd eventually grow up and come home. He's come home, all right, but he sure hasn't grown up."

Something major must have happened to get her this upset. "What did Hunter do?"

Hanna hesitated. Then shook her head. "I'll let him tell you that. Then you can celebrate the fact that I am finally out of your brother's life—for good."

She turned and fled with those words, setting a pace even faster than earlier.

"Wait! Hanna! Please, can I—"

But when Hanna ignored her and kept moving, Savannah didn't try to stop her again. She could understand the other woman's resentment and had to admit that she was in the wrong in this case. She should have given Hanna White a whole lot more credit from the start.

Discouraged, she headed for the bar. She wondered what Hunter would have to say for himself this time.

The Lonesome Spur—like most bars and pubs—wasn't big on windows. Savannah stood in the doorway for a bit, blinking to get used to the subdued lighting.

The bar was in the center of the oblong space. To the right was a pool table, to the left about a dozen tables, most of them vacant.

It was a Monday evening, after all.

Above the bar was a single spur, nailed to the wall.

The lonesome spur was reputed to have belonged to Guy Weadick, a cowboy from Rochester, New York, who'd moved to Canada and started the Calgary Stampede.

Why one of Weadick's spurs had ended up in Coffee Creek, Montana, was anyone's guess.

Her brother was perched on a stool at the bar, his head lowered over a pint of beer.

She sat next to him, shaking her head when the bartender noticed her. "I just spoke to Hanna."

"She stood still long enough for you to do that?"

"Hardly," she admitted. "What happened?"

Hunter took a long swallow of the beer. "I got called in to talk to that Rex Harris, is what happened. What a bastard."

"Was your lawyer present?"

"That kid wouldn't have been any help."

"What are you talking about? Did you even go to the meeting I set up for you?"

"Yeah, I went. But one look at the guy and I knew I was wasting my time."

Savannah groaned.

"Don't give me that. I know what I'm doing."

"So what happened after that?"

"I met Hanna for lunch at Monahan's. It's like Harris knew I would be there. He was stalking the place, waiting for me, and then he drove me to his office in Lewistown and made me give a statement."

Harris sure had been busy today. Already he had statements from the two key players of that night.

"And what did you tell him? Did you stick to the facts the way B.J. laid them out this morning?"

Her brother gave her a testing look. "I told the truth, is what I did. You probably won't like it, now that you're sleeping with B.J. But I had to do it."

"What do you mean I won't like it? Didn't B.J. get it right this morning? Wasn't that the way it really happened?"

She dreaded her brother's answer, sensing he was right and that she wouldn't like it.

"He was trying to get me to cover for him, damn it." Hunter finished his beer, then nodded for another. "You?" he asked his sister.

"No. I'm staying sober, since you're going to need a ride home." So much for her date with B.J. They'd be going home in separate vehicles tonight. She glanced at the door, wondering why he hadn't joined her yet. He must have paid the bill by now.

She put a hand on her brother's arm. "Tell me what you told the state investigator today."

"It's like this. B.J. and I were the first to go into the barn. He went up to check out the loft. I stayed down below waiting for our friends to join us."

"Are you sure?"

"Yup. Then the storm started with an almighty bang of thunder. I saw our friends drive off in the rain and yelled at B.J. that we'd better get moving, too."

Savannah was in shock. Was he telling the truth? She and Hunter were twins, yet she couldn't tell. He *seemed* to be sincere.

"But B.J. said neither one of you went into the loft."

"Look, did you want me to tell the investigator the truth? Or the story B.J. asked me to tell?"

"The truth."

"That's what I did."

Savannah stared at him, trying to decide if this could possibly be the truth. It didn't take long to make up her mind.

No. She just couldn't believe it.

Chapter 14

"Hunter, this is serious. You must tell the truth." Savannah leaned closer toward her brother, wanting to see directly in his eyes.

"I am. It was Sheriff Smith and Bob Lambert who made up those lies. Of course they were protecting B.J. You think they'd have worried about protecting me?"

Savannah got an uneasy feeling in her gut.

Hunter had a point.

"But I can't see B.J. leaving that barn, knowing a man was up in the loft."

"Oh. But you can see *me* doing something like that, huh? Thanks a lot, sis." He signaled the bartender again, and she noticed that his second glass was already empty.

"Slow down on that," she cautioned. "And to answer your question, no, I do not think you would do that. But I do think, as a kid, you might have panicked and made a mistake."

"That's what that Rex Harris said when he tried to trick me into admitting I knew what the watch looked like."

She was relieved to hear that he hadn't fallen for Harris's ploy. Then she felt guilty. If Hunter was innocent, he wouldn't have been able to describe the watch, anyway.

"Look, Hunter. If that's what happened, then of course I support you." He was her brother. And that came before any job. "But why did you fight with Hanna?"

He shook his head. "I can't talk about that."

He chugged back some more beer and she felt sick, thinking about the many long nights their father had spent in this establishment.

"Come home. Getting plastered isn't going to help anything."

He shook her hand off his arm. "Stop trying to mother me. I'll be fine. After a day like I've had, a man is entitled to a few drinks."

"A few? You've already had three." When he ignored this, she tried another approach. "Then give me your keys. I'll drive your truck home and you can call me when you're ready for a ride. It doesn't matter what time. I'll come and get you."

"You're acting like a mother again, Vanna. Give it a rest."

"I'm not acting like your mother. I'm acting like the sheriff. Give me the keys, unless you want to end up spending the night in a cell."

That got his attention. Wordlessly he pulled out his truck keys from his pocket and set them on the bar. She picked them up, hesitated, then left without another word.

It was almost dark outside now. She could see B.J. across the street, leaning against the hood of his vehicle. He had his long legs crossed, and his posture was nice and relaxed, as if he had all the time in the world to wait for her.

"I thought you were going to come into the saloon?"

"I figured it might be better to let you talk to your brother alone. Is he okay?"

Her heart lurched at the concern in his voice. This was so mixed-up. How could she tell him what Hunter had just told her?

It was going to change everything.

She avoided the arm B.J. extended to her, pretending she hadn't seen it. "Rex Harris called him in today, too."

"To get his statement?" B.J.'s eyes were sharp now.

"Yes."

"And? Did it go okay?"

"Not really." She sighed. "B.J., I don't know how to put this."

"Spit it out, woman."

She could see the worry and distrust gathering in his expression as he crossed his arms over his chest and waited to hear what she had to say.

She took a deep breath, then let the words spill out, exactly the way Hunter had told her.

B.J. let out some choice swear words. "So he's putting it all on me now? And let me guess. You believe his version."

She wouldn't go that far. But she couldn't *not* believe it, either. "He's my brother, B.J. I'm all he's got."

"I can't believe this. You're bailing on me. Again." B.J. ground out the words as if each one was bitter and distasteful.

"I'm not. At least, I don't want to. Can't you see how impossible this situation is from my point of view?"

"Sorry, sweetheart. I'm too busy seeing this from my point of view. Which might well be the county jail if your brother gets his way."

"B.J.—"

He turned his back on her and got into the driver's seat. Through the open window he said, "I imagine you can get a lift home with Hunter?"

She nodded, not bothering to explain the arrangement she'd made with her twin.

B.J. took off without another word, laying a little rubber on the road as he hit the gas and making it clear what he thought of her now.

B.J. was too angry to sleep. Too angry to go to the office and focus on paperwork. Almost too angry to breathe.

He sped down Big Valley Road, taking the turns faster than he ought to. Only when the sweep of his headlights picked up the white cross that marked the spot where his brother Brock had been killed almost a year ago did he ease up on the gas.

He was being reckless. Stupid.

Better slow down and make it home safe. An accident wasn't going to solve anything.

But when he got to the turnoff to his family ranch, he went right, instead of left. He drove past Maddie Turner's farmhouse, too, spotting Jackson's truck parked next to Maddie's run-down old wreck.

Good. He was glad that his foster brother

was keeping his aunt company now. That situation had turned out for the best.

If only it hadn't required him to commit to staying on the family ranch. Because the way he felt right now, he was itching to get back on the circuit. A few rounds on the back of an ornery bronc was just what he needed.

B.J. stopped at the dirt access road that led to the Turners' old barn. The so-called scene of the crime. Why had he been such a fool as to think he could win Savannah's heart by protecting her brother?

Now he'd lost everything.

Not just the woman he loved, but possibly his own reputation, to boot.

Any way he looked at the situation, it seemed bleak. Maybe it was time he faced reality. He and Savannah were just not meant to be together.

And as for Hunter—well—he was going to have to play that one by ear. Right now he wanted to drive back to town, pull the big liar out of the bar and beat him to a pulp.

But wouldn't that make him look good in the eyes of the law?

Besides, he couldn't do it to Savannah. Hurting her brother would hurt her, too.

Which was, after all, why he was in this mess in the first place.

* * *

The next morning B.J. figured he should find himself a good lawyer. Instead, he worked out in the barn for several hours, then put in a long day at the office, studying the breeding lines for the various stallions and calculating how much he could afford to spend on a new stud come the fall horse sales.

He avoided his mother and Corb as much as he could, turning down offers for breakfast and lunch. An hour before dinner, he decided to head to town so he wouldn't have to come up with an excuse not to eat another meal with one of them.

Soon enough he'd have to tell them about the mess he was in.

But he wasn't ready yet.

He grabbed a burger at the saloon, looked around for Hunter, intending to have a man-to-man chat with his former friend. He'd cooled off enough now that he thought he could manage to talk this out rather than beat the man senseless.

But Hunter wasn't in town this evening, and after he'd finished his burger, he decided he'd better leave rather than give in to the temptation to get good and drunk.

Out on the street he was surprised to run into Vince Butterfield. Since he'd quit drinking and taken the job as baker at the Cinnamon Stick, the former rodeo star had been a reformed man.

Tonight, though, it seemed as though he was fighting his demons.

B.J. asked him if he had time to get a coffee.

"Nothing open at this time for coffee," Vince replied, his eyes on the front door of the Lonesome Spur.

"Then let me drive you home. We can put your bike in the back." He nodded at the mountain bike that Vince used as his sole method of transport since losing his automobile license in a DUI.

Enough years had passed that Vince could have reapplied for his license, but he claimed that the bike was good enough for him now.

"Hell, B.J. It's like you knew I had trouble on my mind this evening."

"You're not the only one, buddy," B.J. said as he loaded the bike into the back. "Get in. I hope you have some mighty good coffee at your place."

"Sure do. Got some fine cinnamon buns to go with it, too. Maybe you can take another half dozen to Maddie for me. Drop them by on your way home."

They were on the country road now, the

smattering of lights that constituted the town of Coffee Creek just tiny dots in his rear-view mirror. "Why don't you take them to her yourself?"

"Aw—she don't want to see me."

"You sure about that?"

Vince scratched the side of his face. "I'm not so sure I could handle seeing her, either. It's so damn unfair that she got that cancer. Your aunt is one fine woman, B.J. You don't know her well enough to appreciate that fact, but it's true. She may look all rough-and-tumble on the outside, but in her heart, she's all class."

"If that's true, then I don't think she'd blame you for a choice you made forty years ago."

Vince made no comment to that.

Five minutes later, they'd arrived at the trailer that Vince called home. Inside, the place was surprisingly neat, and Vince brewed up a nice, strong pot of coffee, with the promised fresh buns to go with it.

B.J. didn't feel much like eating. But the coffee felt good going down. Not as soothing as a shot of whiskey, but almost.

"Is Maddie the reason you were tempted to fall off the wagon tonight?" he asked Vince.

No sense beating around the bush. The old cowboy would appreciate the direct approach.

"It hurts me to know she's suffering. Just one night, I'd like to forget." Vince stared out the window into the dark. "But I'm glad you came along to drag me out of my misery. I don't want to be the man I was before. But sometimes it's hard standing on your own two feet."

"Don't I know it."

"You got trouble with the sheriff again?"

"When don't I?" It never had been easy with her. And yet, when it worked, it was so damn good.

"You better sort it out," Vince said. "Or you're going to end up an old man like me with nothing but regrets."

Savannah worked the cattle-rustling case hard on Tuesday, phoning neighbors and cattle barns, on the lookout for any sales involving Black Angus yearlings. She knew that the more time passed, the less likely the chance that Kincaid's cattle would be returned to him.

Most every law-abiding citizen in Montana despised cattle rustlers. It went against the code of the land to sneak behind your neighbor's back and make off with cattle that didn't belong to you.

These days, times were hard, and the loss of each calf was significant to a rancher. It was a low-down person who would steal from people who worked so hard for their living.

She was in a foul mood when she arrived home on Tuesday night. Everything she saw reminded her of B.J.—the missing trucks, the mown fields, the tangled sheets on her bed that she hadn't bothered to make that morning…

Impossible to believe they'd spent the night together just forty-eight hours ago. And now he pretty much despised her.

She went into the kitchen, expecting to see her brother. But all she saw was a sink full of dirty dishes.

She found Hunter at the computer in the dining room, playing some dumb war game.

"Jeez, Hunter. Have you wasted the entire day with that?"

Her brother, unshaven and dressed in jeans but no shirt, gave her a brief glance. While continuing to operate the computer controls with his good arm he said, "That investigator asked me to stay in town for a few days, but when he gives me the green light I'll be back on the rodeo circuit."

She looked at him, not knowing what to say. "What about your arm?"

"Oh, it'll be better before you know it."

"Hunter, you can't be a rodeo cowboy forever. Have you given any thought to another career? Maybe you could apply to work on one of the ranches in the area."

"I'd rather get on with Monahan and teach some of his rodeo classes. But with Hanna and me on the outs, I doubt he'd hire me— Oh, damn!"

He slapped the hand of his uninjured arm on the table. It seemed the game had ended and he had lost.

"Well, it's worth a try. In the meantime, while you're staying here I'd appreciate it if you cleaned up after yourself. Maybe even get dinner started in the evening. You do know how to cook, right?" He'd been on his own long enough that he ought to.

"Yeah, I can cook a few things. And I didn't play computer games *all* day. I also did my laundry."

"Well, good for you." She went back into the kitchen. "What do you want to eat?"

She didn't hear his answer, if he gave one. She was too busy wondering when Rex Harris would give her brother permission to leave town. Would Hunter really go back to the rodeo circuit?

And what about B.J.? Was he going to be charged with anything? She didn't see how he could, when it all boiled down to one man's word against another's. Still, the damage to a person's reputation could be costly enough.

The next day she was thrilled to get a lead on the cow-rustling case. A sales yard manager all the way in Bozeman had noticed the Bar K brand on a couple of yearlings brought in by a man they hadn't done business with before.

Savannah got one of her deputies to drive out to Bozeman with her. Curtis Yarrow wasn't one of her favorite employees. He was older, had worked for Sheriff Smith and had been obviously less than excited about shifting allegiance to a female boss.

But Curtis provided the solid backup she needed, and by nightfall, everything was settled. She'd driven the patrol truck down to Bozeman, and when Curtis headed for the driver's seat for the return trip, she didn't argue.

For a while they discussed the events of the day, the desperation and stupidity of the thieves and their relief that they'd found Kincaid's cattle. They fell silent every time a call came through on the radio, but the calls were all routine and nothing that involved their jurisdiction.

Ten minutes from Coffee Creek, Curtis cleared his throat. "I hear a state investigator's been assigned that old case involving your brother."

"Yeah. Rex Harris is the one in charge. He should do a good job."

Curtis gave her a sideways glance. "They say B. J. Lambert is taking the fall for Hunter."

His comment seared Savannah like a branding iron. But she held on to her anger, tamping it down until she could speak without raising her voice. "Oh? And who is saying that?"

Curtis shrugged. "Just people."

"It's not up to us to speculate. It's Harris's job to sort out the facts. Obviously I'm staying out of it."

"Obviously."

It seemed to her that Curtis's comment came with a sneer of sarcasm, but she didn't call him on it. She'd rather people say stuff like this to her face than behind her back.

But unfortunately, it seemed there were plenty of people doing both.

B.J.'s version of the facts might clear her brother in the eyes of the law, but the family reputation was more soiled than ever.

At the office, Savannah checked her messages before heading for home. It was past eight o'clock and she was tired, hungry and dispirited. It seemed that no matter how good she was at her job, she couldn't stop people from gossiping about her and her family.

Her mood lifted, though, when she saw a second car parked next to Hunter's truck in the driveway. Regan was back!

She found her sister, Murray and Hunter on the front porch, drinking beer and eating nachos. Savannah ran right for her sister and gave her a big hug. "You're home!"

"Yup. Sooner than expected."

Had she and Murray fought? But they both seemed happy. Come to think of it, even Hunter had a smug smile on his face.

"What's going on?" She looked from one sibling to the other. "There's something you're not telling me."

Regan held up her smartphone. "I got an email from the University of Washington two days ago."

"Really?" It could mean only one thing. "They accepted you into med school?"

"Sure did," Murray said, sounding proud. "Soon as she found out, Regan turned the car around and headed home."

"Looks like I'm going to need every dime I can earn, after all." Regan had such a big grin on her face that Savannah realized it had been unfair of her to assume that her little sister had given up on her dream.

She'd just been afraid of not getting the one thing she wanted more than anything else in the world. And so she'd run off on a trip and tried to pretend it didn't matter that much.

Oh, how Savannah could relate to that.

"Well, let's celebrate!"

"We already are." Hunter held up his beer can.

"Hang on. I have something even better." She'd bought a bottle of bubbly back in the winter when Regan had first sent out her applications. Back then, Savannah had assumed an acceptance at all three universities was a given.

Instead, they'd gone through months of endless waiting followed by the agonizing disappointment of two refusals.

But none of that mattered now. Her sister was going to med school!

An hour later, the bottle of bubbly was gone, along with the nachos and several frozen pizzas. Some of the elation was starting to fade, as well.

"I've been going through the numbers," Regan said. "I'm going to have to apply for a lot of loans."

"No, you won't." Savannah told her siblings about her plan. She was going to sell the property and divide up the proceeds.

"But if we sell this place, where will you live?" Regan asked.

"I'll rent someplace. Probably not here. I'd like to try a different county. Maybe I'll follow you to Washington."

Regan's eyes narrowed. "But you love it here."

"I love being a sheriff. It doesn't have to be here."

"But people know you in Coffee Creek. How will you get elected if you go somewhere new?"

"Then I'll get hired somewhere as a deputy. Work my way up."

"But you've already done that! I don't understand why you'd want to start at the bottom again."

"Because of me, that's why." Hunter slammed a beer bottle on the porch railing. "She's afraid she won't get reelected because people think I killed that kid in the barn."

"But that was forever ago." Regan had been a kid back then. But she obviously remembered.

"A watch turned up on eBay," Savannah explained to her sister. "It led to a private investigator identifying the body of the man who died in the fire. So now the case has been reopened. I doubt that there's enough evidence to lay charges. But people are talking. Wondering how that boy ended up in that loft."

Regan turned disbelieving eyes to her older brother.

"It was B. J. Lambert," Hunter insisted. "He lured the kid out there so he could steal his watch and wallet. And then he set the fire. He did it all, but still everyone in this damn town blames me."

"I don't understand." Regan looked to Savannah to explain, but she just shrugged. None of this sat right with her. But how could she call her own brother out as a liar? She hadn't been there. She wished to God she had been.

"I think Vanna has the right idea," Hunter mumbled. "We should all leave this town and never look back."

Chapter 15

Thursday afternoon, as he crested a hill about a quarter mile from the barn, B.J. could see the patrol car parked by the house. Two figures were standing next to the car, apparently in conversation.

Griff rode up beside him. "That doesn't look good."

"No, it doesn't." B.J. urged Big Black forward, and Griff and Jay followed with their mounts, half a head behind him. They'd just finished moving the mares and their offspring to the summer grazing pastures.

B.J. had been looking forward to barbecuing a big steak for dinner.

But he guessed that wasn't going to happen.

The two people by the patrol car had spotted them and were now walking toward the home barn. It didn't take long for B.J. to make out his petite mother. The short, barrel-chested man beside her was Rex Harris.

B.J. swore.

At the barn, the three men dismounted. Jay came up to him and offered to take care of Big Black. "Seems like you have other matters to tend to."

B.J. couldn't argue with that. He handed over the reins with a nod of thanks and went around the barn to where his mother and Rex were waiting.

Rex stepped forward. "Son, I'm afraid I have to bring you in for more questioning."

B.J. bristled at being called "son" by a man a mere ten years older than he was. "I already gave my statement."

"Unfortunately, it contradicts the statement given by the only other man there that night."

"This is outrageous." Olive was steaming mad. The high color on her cheekbones suggested she'd been arguing with Rex for some time now. Her eyes fairly snapped as she looked from Rex to B.J. "Obviously Hunter Moody is lying."

"Someone has the truth a little mixed-up,"

Rex agreed. "But I still need to talk to your son."

Olive gave B.J. a look of frustration. He could imagine what was going on in her mind...*this is what happens when you fraternize with people like the Moodys.* But what she actually said was "I've already called a lawyer. Don't talk to this man until he gets here."

"We can wait for the lawyer at the courthouse," Rex said. "B.J., I'll need you to come with me now."

B.J. was sore and tired after a long day of riding. He was so dusty he could feel the grit every time he closed his eyes. "Give me ten minutes to shower first. I've been out riding since seven this morning."

Rex hesitated. Maybe he was thinking how bad his car would smell if he didn't say yes, because finally he nodded. "Ten more minutes won't hurt, I guess. You go ahead. I'll wait in the car."

Savannah went home a few hours early on Thursday. She had an appointment with the Realtor who had contacted her on behalf of Sam O'Neil. She'd given herself time to tidy up the place before the woman arrived.

There were no cars in the driveway when

she drove up to her home. She had no idea where Hunter could be, but she knew Regan was working. Regan had texted her earlier with the good news that Straws had given both her and Murray their jobs back. Not only that but he'd also agreed to schedule her for extra hours to make up for the money she'd lost by taking her trip.

Savannah was happy for her sister, and very proud. At least life was going in the right direction for one member of the Moody family. Really, it was all she had the right to ask for.

So why did she feel so crappy?

She was just being selfish. She'd be fine starting over in a new place. As for B.J.— she'd survived eighteen years without him. She could do it again.

But it wouldn't be easy. She wondered what he was doing right now.

Was he thinking of her? Did he miss her?

Not likely. In his mind she'd betrayed him by not believing his version of the facts over her brother. Which wasn't fair. If he'd wanted her to believe him, then he should have told her the truth from the beginning.

Something, she was sure, he still hadn't done.

She sighed as she opened the back door,

and her bad mood totally tanked when she saw the state of the kitchen.

The place was a disaster. Hunter had obviously made omelets for breakfast. He'd used every bowl in the kitchen, and there were bits of grated cheese and chopped onion scattered on the floor. Some of the raw-egg mixture had spilled and cooked onto the stove. And the dirty frying pan was sitting in the sink on top of a stack of dishes.

Great. She had a little less than two hours before the Realtor showed up and she hadn't counted on spending all that time in the kitchen.

Savannah tackled the dirty dishes first, then the dining room and living area. Her room was fine—she'd made the bed that morning—but her basket of laundry was overflowing. She carried it downstairs, intending to start a load of whites. But the washing machine was full of damp clothing.

Hunter's, of course.

She tried to transfer them to the dryer, but it was stuffed, too. Damn it, couldn't her brother do anything around here?

Savannah folded his dry clothes for him, then stuck the wet ones in and started the machine. Within a few seconds an annoying clanking sound made it clear that he hadn't emptied his pockets of all his change.

She opened the dryer door and searched for the offending item.

Sure enough, it was a coin. But a foreign-looking gold one.

Savannah leaned against the dryer, suddenly feeling weak and very, very foolish. This coin was just like the one B.J. had found in the loft the day they'd given the old barn a good search. She still had that coin in the evidence room at work.

She made her way upstairs and out to the porch, where she sank into a wicker chair and tried to think.

But there was only one way Hunter could have got his hands on this coin.

She lifted her head at the sound of an approaching vehicle. She was expecting to see the Realtor. But it was Hunter's old truck. Her brother parked, then stepped out with a swagger. She noticed his cast was off. He'd been to the doctor.

"Good as new," he said, flexing his arm as he headed toward the porch. He paused when he saw the expression on her face.

She held out the coin for him to see.

"You found my lucky coin. Hey, thanks."

He went to take it from her, but she snatched it away.

"Where did you get this, Hunter?"

Something dark, like fear or dread, flashed in his eyes. And then he was grinning again. "Hell if I can remember. I've had that thing forever. It's brought me lots of good luck on the rodeo circuit. I never ride without it." He reached out again. "Give it back."

She hesitated. She could give him this coin and never say a word about it to anyone.

They could carry on with their plan. Regan off to be a doctor, her working as a deputy, maybe somewhere close to Regan in Seattle. And Hunter riding the circuit again.

She didn't think B.J. would end up being prosecuted for arson or the death of Travis McBride. There wasn't enough evidence. Even if there were, with B.J.'s good reputation and the Lamberts' ability to hire a top attorney, he'd get off for sure.

But how far was she willing to go to protect her brother?

Was being respectable only a matter of what other people thought of you?

Or what you thought of yourself?

Savannah closed her fist over the coin. Then tucked it into the front pocket of her jeans.

"What the hell are you doing?" Hunter grabbed her shoulder, hard enough to hurt.

She shook him off. "Forget it, Hunter. I'm onto you. Really, I knew a lot earlier—I just didn't want to admit it."

"Don't say that."

"You let B.J. take all the blame.... Was he even there when you took that coin?"

Hunter hesitated, then admitted, "No."

She stared at him, appalled, and yet not surprised. She thought back to the day her brother had given his statement to the investigator. "That's why you and Hanna fought, isn't it? She found out you'd lied to Rex Harris. And she wanted you to tell the truth."

"She guessed I didn't tell the truth. And she was mad that I wouldn't level with her."

"Was B.J. a part of any of it? Did he know about the guy in the loft?"

Disgust flashed over her brother's face. And shame. "No."

"So he was completely innocent?"

"Look. I'm not proud of what happened. But I didn't know, okay? I thought that kid was dead."

With that comment, Hunter had her completely confused. "Why would Travis have been dead?"

"Hell." Hunter's hands were fists. "I'll tell you, okay? But this is just between you and me."

She wanted to stop him right there. He could say this was just between the two of them, but she wasn't only his sister. She was the sheriff of this county.

Which meant she had to get at the truth. Whatever way she could.

"You'd better be telling the truth this time, Hunter."

He took a deep breath. "I met Travis Mc-Bride online. It was like a chat room for guys who were interested in rodeo. I was training a lot back then and had done good at some junior competitions. He asked if I could teach him how to ride bucking broncos. I said I would if he could get to Montana."

"So that's what he was doing here. June Savage couldn't figure out why a kid from California would run away to Montana."

"He wanted to be a cowboy. So I snuck him into Monahan's and we practiced on some of their horses. Out in the far pasture, where no one could see us. He needed a place to shack up for the night, and I told him about the old barn on Silver Creek Ranch. That's when I got the idea of having a party out there. I dropped Travis off first. Told him I'd be back with some friends. He should hide up in the loft and make spooky sounds—give the girls a good scare."

This sounded like one of Hunter's usual pranks. But when had he crossed the line? When had prank turned into crime? "So then what happened?"

"I left him with a bottle of vodka that I'd lifted from—well, you don't need to know that part. Then I went back to organize my friends. We decided to drive up to the barn in ATVs since the road was so rough. B.J. and me led the way."

"But the prank didn't work the way you planned?"

"No." Hunter's shoulders slumped. "B.J. and I got there first. The barn was all quiet. I didn't know what Travis was doing—he should have heard us drive up and been making scary noises."

"So what did you do?"

"I figured Travis must have gotten bored and run off, maybe hitched a ride back to town. I went up the loft to make sure, but he was there, all right, only out cold."

Sweat glistened on her brother's brow now. He rubbed his hands on his jeans and took another deep breath.

"The bottle of vodka was beside him. Almost empty. And he wasn't moving. It seemed like he wasn't even breathing, either. I panicked, figured he'd died of alcohol poisoning. And it was my fault."

"Let me get this straight," Savannah said. She was sweating, too, now. "You really believed Travis was dead?"

"I was positive."

"But did you check his vital signs?"

"I tried. But I didn't know what I was doing. It seemed like he wasn't breathing. And I couldn't find a pulse. I grabbed the bottle and hid it in my jacket. I took his wallet, too, so he couldn't be identified. His watch looked expensive, so I grabbed that and a weird coin he had in his pocket."

"There were actually two weird coins in his pocket. B.J. found the other one when we went to check out the barn a few weeks ago."

Hunter looked surprised. "Hell. I must have missed it."

"So you stole Tyler's ID and his possessions, and then what?"

Hunter flinched at the word *stole*. "I wasn't wanting any of that stuff. I was just worried that they would be clues that would get me in trouble. I was panicked, big-time. And then the lightning struck and the barn was on fire.

There wasn't time to do anything. B.J. and I had to run for our lives."

Savannah couldn't believe Hunter had been so foolish. "You didn't even try to save the boy in the loft?"

"How many times do I have to tell you? I thought he was dead. And I was terrified. I figured the old barn with all that hay inside would go up in a flash."

Hunter stopped talking then, and for a long while neither one said anything. Savannah didn't know whether to scream or cry from mortification and regret.

All along B.J. had known that Hunter had been up in the loft and must have seen the boy.

But he'd covered for him.

To think she'd blamed B.J. for that night, when she should have been on her knees, thanking him.

"This is what's going to happen. We're going out to Coffee Creek Ranch and you're going to apologize to B.J. Then we're going to town and you're giving Harris another statement. The truth this time."

"Are you crazy? We have a plan. You said so yourself. We have to think of the future."

"There is no future for any of us if we don't

do the right thing now. Get in my vehicle, Hunter. We're going now."

"No bloody way. What I told you was just between the two of us."

"You really expect me to keep everything you said a secret? And let B.J. take the fall?"

"He's willing to do it. And you know damn well his family has the money to protect him."

Hunter had disappointed her many times over the years. But she'd always hoped that at the core, he was a good, if misguided person. But how could she believe that now, when he was saying these awful things? "Please, Hunter. Don't make me get my gun and force you to come with me."

"You would never do that."

"Don't put me to the test."

But then he was running, out the door and into his truck. She had time to get her gun, but just stood on the porch watching as he drove away.

He was right. She couldn't shoot at her own brother, not even to aim at one of his truck tires.

But there was something else she would do. Something she *had* to do.

It was late afternoon when Savannah drove up to Coffee Creek Ranch, having texted the

Realtor to reschedule their appointment. She pulled up to the main house, but before she had time to turn off the ignition, Olive Lambert was marching out of the front door and up to her truck. She stopped about a foot from the driver's-side door.

Since Olive hadn't left enough room for Savannah to open the door, she lowered the window.

"What are *you* doing here?" Olive wasn't bothering with the pleasantries today.

"I need to talk to B.J."

"Then you ought to be in town. That's where that special investigator took him for questioning. Such stuff and nonsense. We both know who the authorities ought to be harassing. And it isn't my son."

Olive's eyes were brilliantly green and flashing anger.

This time, Savannah couldn't blame her.

"Rex Harris was here?"

Olive nodded.

"When?"

"About an hour ago."

"Thanks, Mrs. Lambert." She raised the window, then waited for Olive to move a safe distance away before she turned her SUV around and headed back to town.

This was much worse than she'd expected.

What was B.J. saying to Harris? And why hadn't he got word to her that he'd been hauled in for questioning?

Chapter 16

Savannah made it as far as the receptionist's office at the courthouse before being asked to take a seat and wait for Mr. Harris, who was in a meeting.

"If he's meeting with Mr. B. J. Lambert, then I need to see both of them." Savannah didn't sit, expecting that she would be called into the meeting room right away.

She was correct. The receptionist returned quickly and ushered her into an interview room, where Harris was sitting with June Savage, an older man in a suit and tie who had to be a lawyer—and B.J.

B.J.'s broad shoulders, cowboy hat and sun-bronzed skin looked out of place in the office setting. He appeared tired and frustrated, but not cowed, and he nodded slightly to acknowledge her presence.

He didn't smile, though. Not even a little. And Savannah's guilt was overwhelming at the sight of the man who had been her friend—and her lover—enduring an interrogation that he didn't deserve.

The four of them were sitting at a table with room for eight, the polished wood surface littered with mugs of coffee, a plate of cookies and lots of loose paper.

Savannah looked from Harris, to B.J., then back to Harris.

"My brother just told me what really happened the night of the fire. You need to release B.J., locate Hunter and bring him in to revise his statement. You'll find that B.J. is exonerated in every way. The party was never his idea. He'd never met Travis McBride before, never stole the watch and certainly didn't go up in the loft area the night of the fire. My brother's revised statement will clear him entirely."

Everyone around the table looked stunned. Except B.J.

"Do you know what you're doing, Savannah?" His voice was laced with caution.

"You should have told me the truth. From the beginning."

He averted his eyes.

"I know. You were trying to protect me by protecting Hunter." He was just so noble... that was his biggest strength and also his biggest flaw.

"Are you saying your brother lied in his previous statement?" Harris spoke slowly, seeking absolute clarity with this.

"Yes."

"How refreshing to get a straight answer for a change."

By Harris's dry tone, Savannah gathered that B.J. had been giving him the runaround.

Why not tell the truth and protect himself?

He wasn't giving Harris a hard time for Hunter's sake, that was for sure. He'd done it for her. And how had she repaid him? By throwing him to the lions to save her brother.

"I wish Hunter were here to tell you himself," she said.

"Since he isn't, we have only your word that B.J. had no involvement."

"My word and this." She took out the coin and handed it to Harris.

She told them the entire story, from the moment her brother had met Travis McBride online and promised to train him to be a cowboy, to the awful ending, where he had stripped the passed-out young man of his wallet, coins and whiskey bottle.

"It looks like an old British coin," Harris said. "Where did you find it?"

"In the dryer today, at the bottom of a load of my brother's clothes. I have another just like it in the evidence room at my office. B.J. and I found it a few weeks ago in the loft of the old barn."

"Looks like something that belongs in a coin collection," Harris said, passing the coin to the private investigator.

"Tyler's father is a numismatist," June said. "Tyler may have stolen the coins hoping to sell them at some point. His father said he'd done this before."

"My brother has carried that coin as some sort of talisman all these years. When he saw that I'd found it, he confessed the whole story to me. I couldn't convince him to come here and revise his statement. But I'm hoping—"

There was a tap on the door, and then the receptionist stepped inside. "I'm sorry to interrupt again. But I have a Hunter Moody and his friend Hanna White, who insist they have something urgent to say to Mr. Harris."

And then her brother and Hanna were in the room.

Savannah felt suddenly weak—whether from relief or fear she wasn't sure. Maybe both. Somehow B.J. had noticed. He pulled out a chair and urged her to sit.

Meanwhile, everyone else was focused on her brother.

"Your sister just showed us this," Harris said, reclaiming the coin from June.

Hunter's face grew pale, but he didn't back down. "Yeah. It's kind of a long story."

"We've heard it once," Harris said, his voice stern. "But we're more than prepared to sit through it again."

Hunter spoke, mostly without interruption, for forty minutes. All the while, Hanna sat silently beside him, holding his hand. When Hunter finally reached the end of his sordid tale, for a long while no one said anything. Savannah felt as if she might cry—for her brother, who had made so many terrible choices.

And for herself—and what she'd done to a very fine man.

She'd known B.J. was covering for Hunter. And she'd let him.

"You're sure you've told us the truth this time," Rex Harris finally said.

"Yes, sir."

"I'm going to need to see you separately for a while." He glanced at the lawyer. "Maybe you should stay, too. The rest of you leave now. My office will be in touch."

B.J. followed Savannah down the stairs, then out the main doors of the courthouse. The day was on its way to being a real scorcher. First day of July, he remembered. He sure hoped this month would be quieter than the last.

He had never seen Savannah more miserable than she looked right now. He could tell she was on the verge of tears. She kept her head high, though, and seemed determined to go straight to her vehicle and get away as fast as she could.

"Look. I'm really sorry, Savannah."

That stopped her in her tracks. "*You're* sorry? You have been so bloody noble in all of this. You did everything you could to protect him. And you never even *told* me."

He couldn't. He'd wanted to protect *her*.

"No one's going to blame you for something your brother did."

"Why wouldn't they? I blame myself. He didn't have a father or mother providing guidance in his life. I should have kept a closer eye on him."

But they'd been the same age. And she hadn't had the influence of caring parents, either.

Savannah never would cut herself any slack. It wasn't in her nature. And it was one of the reasons he loved her so damn much.

"You'll see," he told her. "When the next election comes around, the people of this community will show how much they support you."

"When the next election comes around, I won't be here."

Her words hit him like a bucket of cold water. "What?"

"I never had a chance to tell you—Regan's been accepted to med school in Seattle. I'm selling our land and moving to Washington, as well. Hopefully I'll get a job in law enforcement and start rebuilding my life."

B.J. couldn't speak at first. Tears were welling in Savannah's eyes. He couldn't believe this was really what she wanted. "What if I don't want you to go?"

"You'll be so much better off when I'm gone. My family has given you nothing but grief."

"Maybe that's true of Hunter. But not you."

"Don't you see? If it hadn't been for me, you would have been free to tell the truth years ago. All this time, you were lying for my sake. How can I forgive myself for causing you all that pain?"

"I don't blame you. You shouldn't, either."

"That's impossible." She swallowed, then blotted her eyes with the back of her hand. "But there's something I need to say first. Something you should know."

He tried to take her hands, but she wouldn't let him.

"I've always been in love with you, B.J. But never more than today when I finally understood what you sacrificed for my family...." She swallowed. "For me."

The words should have sounded so sweet to him. But how could they, when she was crying and looking about as heartbroken as a woman could be?

"I'm sure you've had enough of the Moodys—that you'll never want to see a one of us again. But...I had to tell you how I feel about you. Just so you know how it was. And now I should get going. I have an appointment with a Realtor in half an hour."

What could he say to stop her?

She took a step backward.

"Hang on a minute. Where are you going with this, Savannah? First you tell me you're leaving town. Then that you love me. It's crazy. What good is that supposed to do? Do you want me to move to Washington with you? Because I will."

"You belong here. And you'll be better off without me."

"You really think that?"

"The best thing I can do for you is let you go." She took another step, then turned and ran for her SUV.

"You're damn good at it, too," he shouted after her. But he doubted she heard.

B.J. was mad as hell. Mostly at Hunter. Why hadn't the idiot told him about the kid in the loft? B.J. would have been able to figure out that Travis was passed out, not just unconscious. That death had been totally preventable.

But he'd kept his mouth shut in that room. It was what his lawyer had advised him to do. And anyway, he had no idea what to say. Hunter was about to face the consequences for what he'd done that night.

And so was Savannah.

Did she really love him? Or was it just guilt that had made her say that to him right now? She was taking everything Hunter had done wrong onto her own shoulders.

How could he stop her from doing that?

There had to be some solution. He wasn't the kind of man to give up when he wanted something—someone—this bad.

The for-sale sign at the front of the lane stood out in bold red, white and blue. Long after the agreement had been signed with the Realtor and the sign had been hammered into place, Savannah stood staring at it.

Rather than simply accept the offer from Sam O'Neil, she'd decided to list the property for thirty days to see if she might get a higher price.

It was time for the Moodys to leave Coffee Creek.

She'd cleared out her bank account today, coming up with the retainer for Hunter's lawyer. Mr. Lockhart had stopped in at the house when he'd dropped Hunter off after the meeting with Harris.

He'd said the situation was serious but there were some exonerating circumstances. He was hopeful they could cut a deal and the punishment wouldn't be too severe.

Tomorrow evening, at the town-council meeting, Savannah was going to hand in her resignation. After that, she would look into locating a new care home for her mother in

Seattle and a nearby apartment for her and Regan.

She placed a hand on the for-sale sign and gave it a push to make sure it was in nice and solid. Satisfied, she headed for the house to see if she had any frozen entrées for dinner since Regan was working late.

There were about a dozen men and women present in the city-commission chambers at city hall the next evening, including the mayor, the city manager and the city attorney.

Savannah had been expecting this.

What she hadn't expected to see was B. J. Lambert, sitting in the area reserved for guests.

He was tall, handsome and somber. She hadn't been nervous up to that point, but suddenly her palms were damp and her throat went dry.

Beside B.J. were some other people she recognized. Mr. Kincaid, whose cattle she'd rescued. Beside him were some kids she'd caught spray-painting the sidewalk by her office a few months ago and had roped into community service to atone for their crimes.

There were other faces she recognized, too. Faces from a dozen different cases she'd

worked on over the three years she'd been acting sheriff in this town.

When it came to the time in the meeting
for new business, Savannah stepped forward.
She had her letter of resignation all typed up
and ready to be presented to the chair. She'd
only read the first few lines, though, when
B.J. interrupted her.

"Before you accept the sheriff's letter of
resignation, would you allow me and a few
of the citizens of this county to make a brief
presentation?"

Mayor McCormick, a punctilious man who
worked hard to ensure meetings closed on
time, was surprisingly open to the idea.

It turned out B.J. had a video clip as well
as several spoken testimonials, all commend-
ing her for the great job she was doing as
the sheriff. Some of the people he had on
tape surprised her. Burt from the post office,
Tabitha from the library, Ed from the feed
supply shop…and so many more.

A lot of them were people she could have
sworn were talking behind her back the past
few weeks.

But maybe she'd misunderstood.

Maybe instead of judging her, they'd
merely been feeling sorry about her brother.

That was what this video seemed to be implying.

At the end of the fifteen-minute presentation, the mayor thanked B.J. and B.J. took his seat.

"Are you willing to reconsider your resignation?" the mayor asked.

Tears were coming down her cheeks so fast, all she could do was nod. After this show of faith from her community how could she leave?

Later, B.J. came to find her. Before she could thank him, he asked if she'd heard from her Realtor.

She checked her phone, which she'd turned off for the meeting. Three missed calls, all from the same source. "How did you guess?"

"You've got a bidding war going on for your property."

"You can't know that."

"Yes, I can. I'm one of the prospective buyers."

"Seriously? Are you looking to expand Coffee Creek Ranch? But my land is a fifteen-minute drive from your spread."

"I figure fifteen minutes is a pretty good buffer from my mother. Farther would be better. But then, you've got that pretty view. And that's worth something, too, don't you think?"

He had her so confused. But she liked the way he was looking at her. She hadn't seen him this happy or trouble-free in ages.

"It's the perfect solution. I buy the land from you—Regan has the money for med school, and we get married."

"W-we do?"

He kissed her. "We do. Then we build the home of our dreams. You continue to work as the sheriff and I run the quarter-horse operation at Coffee Creek. Children are optional, but horses aren't. I want to have a few of our own. And dogs. At least two."

"Oh, B.J." He was painting a picture of a perfect life. But was it really possible?

"The people here in Coffee Creek disapprove of what Hunter did. But they love and respect you, Savannah. Not nearly as much as I do, though. Will you stay? And marry me?"

"But Regan. I promised her I'd move to Washington to be near her."

"Talk to her. You might be surprised to find out that she's more ready to leave the nest than you think."

Remembering her sister's excitement to go with Murray on that road trip, Savannah suspected he was probably right.

"Your mother won't be pleased."

"Maybe not. But my aunt Maddie thinks

it's an excellent plan." His eyes glinted with humor. "So does Cassidy. She's talking double wedding this November. What do you think? Or would you rather have the spotlight entirely on you?"

She shook her head.

"I didn't think so."

"A double wedding would be perfect."

"Is that a yes?"

She put her hands on either side of his face. This gorgeous cowboy. Was she really going to get to spend the rest of her life with him? "I love you so much. This feels like a dream. I was so sure you'd be better off without me."

"Never that." He kissed her again, made her feel, right down to her toes, the passion he had for her. "I know marriage is scary. But you give me your best, and I promise to give you mine, too."

She could ask for no better wedding vow. "Yes, I'll marry you." And she kissed him again.

* * * * *

Get 4 FREE REWARDS!

We'll send you 2 FREE Books plus 2 FREE Mystery Gifts.

Harlequin Special Edition books relate to finding comfort and strength in the support of loved ones and enjoying the journey no matter what life throws your way.

FREE Value Over **$20**

Get 4 FREE REWARDS!

We'll send you 2 FREE Books plus 2 FREE Mystery Gifts.

Harlequin Romance Larger-Print books will immerse you in emotion and intimacy simmering in international locales—experience the rush of falling in love!

FREE
Value Over
$20

Get 4 FREE REWARDS!

We'll send you 2 FREE Books plus 2 FREE Mystery Gifts.

FREE Value Over **$20**

Both the **Romance** and **Suspense** collections feature compelling novels written by many of today's bestselling authors.

YES! Please send me 2 FREE novels from the Essential Romance or Essential Suspense Collection and my 2 FREE gifts (gifts are worth about $10 retail). After receiving them, if I don't wish to receive any more books, I can return the shipping statement marked "cancel." If I don't cancel, I will receive 4 brand-new novels every month and be billed just $7.24 each in the U.S. or $7.49 each in Canada. That's a savings of up to 28% off the cover price. It's quite a bargain! Shipping and handling is just 50¢ per book in the U.S. and $1.25 per book in Canada.* I understand that accepting the 2 free books and gifts places me under no obligation to buy anything. I can always return a shipment and cancel at any time. The free books and gifts are mine to keep no matter what I decide.

Choose one: ☐ **Essential Romance** (194/394 MDN GQ6M) ☐ **Essential Suspense** (191/391 MDN GQ6M)

Name (please print)

Address   Apt. #

City   State/Province   Zip/Postal Code

Email: Please check this box ☐ if you would like to receive newsletters and promotional emails from Harlequin Enterprises ULC and its affiliates. You can unsubscribe anytime.

> Mail to the **Reader Service:**
> **IN U.S.A.:** P.O. Box 1341, Buffalo, NY 14240-8531
> **IN CANADA:** P.O. Box 603, Fort Erie, Ontario L2A 5X3

Want to try 2 free books from another series! Call 1-800-873-8635 or visit www.ReaderService.com.

Get 4 FREE REWARDS!

We'll send you 2 FREE Books plus <u>2</u> FREE Mystery Gifts.

Harlequin Heartwarming Larger-Print books will connect you to uplifting stories where the bonds of friendship, family and community unite.

FREE Value Over **$20**

YES! Please send me 2 FREE Harlequin Heartwarming Larger-Print novels and my 2 FREE mystery gifts (gifts worth about $10 retail). After receiving them, if I don't wish to receive any more books, I can return the shipping statement marked "cancel." If I don't cancel, I will receive 4 brand-new larger-print novels every month and be billed just $5.74 per book in the U.S. or $6.24 per book in Canada. That's a savings of at least 21% off the cover price. It's quite a bargain! Shipping and handling is just 50¢ per book in the U.S. and $1.25 per book in Canada.* I understand that accepting the 2 free books and gifts places me under no obligation to buy anything. I can always return a shipment and cancel at any time. The free books and gifts are mine to keep no matter what I decide.

161/361 HDN GNPZ

Name (please print)

Address   Apt. #

City   State/Province   Zip/Postal Code

Email: Please check this box ☐ if you would like to receive newsletters and promotional emails from Harlequin Enterprises ULC and its affiliates. You can unsubscribe anytime.

Mail to the **Reader Service:**
IN U.S.A.: P.O. Box 1341, Buffalo, NY 14240-8531
IN CANADA: P.O. Box 603, Fort Erie, Ontario L2A 5X3

Want to try 2 free books from another series? Call 1-800-873-8635 or visit www.ReaderService.com.

---

*Terms and prices subject to change without notice. Prices do not include sales taxes, which will be charged (if applicable) based on your state or country of residence. Canadian residents will be charged applicable taxes. Offer not valid in Quebec. This offer is limited to one order per household. Books received may not be as shown. Not valid for current subscribers to Harlequin Heartwarming Larger-Print books. All orders subject to approval. Credit or debit balances in a customer's account(s) may be offset by any other outstanding balance owed by or to the customer. Please allow 4 to 6 weeks for delivery. Offer available while quantities last.

Your Privacy—Your information is being collected by Harlequin Enterprises ULC, operating as Reader Service. For a complete summary of the information we collect, how we use this information and to whom it is disclosed, please visit our privacy notice located at corporate.harlequin.com/privacy-notice. From time to time we may also exchange your personal information with reputable third parties. If you wish to opt out of this sharing of your personal information, please visit readerservice.com/consumerschoice or call 1-800-873-8635. **Notice to California Residents**—Under California law, you have specific rights to control and access your data. For more information on these rights and how to exercise them, visit corporate.harlequin.com/california-privacy.

HW20R2

Get 4 FREE REWARDS!

We'll send you 2 FREE Books plus 2 FREE Mystery Gifts.

Harlequin Historical books will seduce you with passion, drama and sumptuous detail of romances set in long-ago eras!

FREE Value Over **$20**

YES! Please send me 2 FREE Harlequin Historical novels and my 2 FREE gifts (gifts are worth about $10 retail). After receiving them, if I don't wish to receive any more books, I can return the shipping statement marked "cancel." If I don't cancel, I will receive 6 brand-new novels every month and be billed just $5.69 per book in the U.S. or $6.24 per book in Canada. That's a savings of at least 12% off the cover price! It's quite a bargain! Shipping and handling is just 50¢ per book in the U.S. and $1.25 per book in Canada.* I understand that accepting the 2 free books and gifts places me under no obligation to buy anything. I can always return a shipment and cancel at any time. The free books and gifts are mine to keep no matter what I decide.

246/349 HDN GNPD

Name (please print)

Address   Apt. #

City   State/Province   Zip/Postal Code

Email: Please check this box ☐ if you would like to receive newsletters and promotional emails from Harlequin Enterprises ULC and its affiliates. You can unsubscribe anytime.

Mail to the **Reader Service:**
IN U.S.A.: P.O. Box 1341, Buffalo, NY 14240-8531
IN CANADA: P.O. Box 603, Fort Erie, Ontario L2A 5X3

Want to try 2 free books from another series? Call 1-800-873-8635 or visit www.ReaderService.com.

Visit
ReaderService.com
Today!

As a valued member of the Harlequin Reader Service, you'll find these benefits and more at ReaderService.com:

- Try 2 free books from any series
- Access risk-free special offers
- View your account history & manage payments
- Browse the latest Bonus Bucks catalog

Don't miss out!

If you want to stay up-to-date on the latest at the Harlequin Reader Service and enjoy more content, make sure you've signed up for our monthly News & Notes email newsletter. Sign up online at ReaderService.com or by calling Customer Service at 1-800-873-8635.

RS20